Confessions of an Erotic Author Part One: The University Years

Confessions of an Erotic Author, Volume 1

P.T. Brown

Published by Guinea Pig Publishing, 2023.

This is a work of fiction. Similarities to real people, places, or events are entirely coincidental.

CONFESSIONS OF AN EROTIC AUTHOR PART ONE: THE UNIVERSITY YEARS

First edition. August 11, 2023.

Written by P.T. Brown.

Also by P.T. Brown

Confessions of an Erotic Author
Confessions of an Erotic Author Part One: The University Years

Four couples get kinky
Four Couples Get Kinky, Part One: Exploration

Mary's Erotic Adventures
Mary's Awakening
Mary's Evolution

Standalone
Sophie's Hotwife Adventures

Watch for more at https://pt-brown.com/.

Table of Contents

Foreword

When I first started writing erotica, I focused on the fictional characters I'd create. First came my four married couples, each into a different aspect of sexual exploration. Their short stories became quite a collection and eventually resulted in a published book. We have since found out they are friends and don't know each other's kinks yet. Cue the saucy second book when secrets are shared.

Then, entirely by chance, a short story about a young university student, Mary, became a much longer piece of published work, had a sequel, and now has another in the works. I love writing Mary, and one afternoon, after I'd written a particularly steamy liaison of hers, I realised why.

Mary represents me at that age. Her story doesn't, but the way I used to think and act flooded out of me onto the page when I was writing her. So with some encouragement from my partner, I started writing me, for me, and as me. What followed started with fiction, but there is truth in here in places.

I've written many "confessions" - not that this is what they are, confessing tends to infer something wrong was done. None of what you read here is wrong, though if you have particularly strong religious beliefs or believe in monogamy, you should probably go no further. I didn't write these stories in chronological order, but they have been presented as such here and will be in my next book to allow things to make sense.

This first book mainly covers my University years, but starts a little earlier, as my boyfriend at that time was a year older than me, so I visited him at his University before I finished school. I leave it entirely to you to decide how much is truth and how much is fiction. I hope you enjoy reading my work.

P. (aka Pixie - later on, at least).

October 2007 – The man of my dreams, his friend, and his friend's girlfriend

I was deliriously happy. I was walking on air to have the boyfriend I had wanted for quite a while. He was a year older than me and popular, so our getting together raised my profile at school, which improved my confidence. He took my virginity — but then I offered it relatively easily, and we had a fabulous sex life, screwing as often as possible. Then, after about twelve amazing months, the day I dreaded came. He headed off to university.

It wasn't a million miles away, but I didn't have a licence, let alone a car. While I desperately missed him, I clung to the knowledge that as soon as he was settled, I could go and visit. A month after he left, he called and asked if I'd like to go and stay with him for the weekend, just days after my eighteenth birthday.

I accepted. Of course, I did.

He said there was a gig at the student union that weekend, and we could go to it on Friday night with all his new friends. A few of their girlfriends were coming to stay, too, so we could make a weekend of it.

I needed to hit the shops. I needed something to wear. Generally, I was your leggings, Dr Martens, and baggy jumper kind of girl, particularly at school. Granted, I'd bought a few things over the last year for our dates, but he always told me how much he liked my look, so I'd just tweaked it a little as my confidence grew. I felt I'd need something a little more "grown-up" for a weekend at a university.

Most of it was easy. I bought tight jeans, some nice tops — not my typical style but hey — and a skirt. The challenge was Friday evening. I hadn't met any of his friends or any other girlfriends. I took a gamble on all of them being a year older than me, at least, but that was all the intel I had.

I decided the best thing to do, was to give him a pleasant surprise, and hope I could hold my own. I chose a dress (he'd never seen me in a dress). It was black lace, with long sleeves (October in the UK!), low cut at the front and even lower at the back. Still, not backless — even I knew student unions weren't that upmarket. It was also devilishly short, not just by my standards but by any standard. Not being one to advertise too much of myself to anyone but my man, I chose some relatively opaque black tights to go with it and some little suede low-heeled boots.

I tried it all together the morning I was due to catch the train to see him. Never in my life would I have called myself hot. But that morning, in that mirror, I saw something in myself that I didn't know was there, and when I saw it, I instantly started to feel a little different.

I was like a child sitting on the train. It was only a few hours but felt like an age, counting the stops until I eventually pulled up at my destination. And there he was, standing on the platform holding a single red rose. I nearly cried.

The kiss on the platform was the missed four weeks of kissing combined into one. Anyone else watching on would have thought we were mad. Maybe we were, but I missed those lips.

We caught the bus to the university from the station. We made it to his room without bumping into anyone he knew on campus. His room was on a long thin corridor with sixteen doors. Fourteen led to small bedrooms, one to a shared kitchen, and the other to a large bathroom with toilets, showers and the like.

Everyone on his floor (the ground floor) was guys, and the identical corridors above were girls. His room was tiny — as expected — with a single bed (all we needed!), a table and a wardrobe.

We sat, and I opened my eighteenth birthday presents. Chocolate — nice, some perfume — nicer, a sexy nightie — nicer still, and for comedy value (he claimed) a dildo — very nice indeed, that made two (the first one he didn't know about — I'd bought it to keep me company when he left for Uni. It helped!

I was just about to open my last present, hiding in his jeans, when the door knocked, and the rest of the afternoon was a procession of his friends either coming to meet me or bringing their girlfriends to meet both of us. I'd been horny for a week, this was annoying, but I handled it.

Many of his friends were good-looking guys, and their girlfriends were beautiful. The hottest and friendliest girlfriend of the bunch was seeing the guy who lived next door to him, Rich. Her name was Jane. She'd been to visit the Uni before and knew her way around. She managed to extract me from the commotion of everyone else coming and going to grab a coffee from the nearest coffee shop on campus.

She was friendly and, as anticipated, older than me, older than most of them, in fact, at twenty-one, confident and rather glamorous. I poured my heart out to her a little about not knowing what to wear, how to fit in and being nervous about the evening ahead. She kindly offered to make Rich change in my boyfriend's room, and we got ready together in his. I jumped at the chance.

Later that evening, I got into my outfit with Jane in Rich's room. Jane looked across from the mirror, applying her makeup, and laughed at me. "And you were worried about fitting in," she said. "You look stunning." It was just the compliment I needed, and I took it happily, no matter how genuine it may have been.

I grabbed my makeup bag and sat in front of the mirror while Jane moved to put on her dress. I wasn't at all surprised at how stunning she looked. I put on my makeup , which was a rarity, looked at myself in the mirror, and sighed.

"What's up?" Jane asked.

"I don't do this often. I'm not exactly an expert," I said, a little deflated.

"You look natural. What were you going for?"

4

"I'd prefer something a little bit more sultry. You know, to go with the black lace and little boots?"

"Mind if I?" She asked, gesturing to her makeup bag.

"No, please, if you don't mind."

A few minutes later, she stepped back, looked at me, and smiled. "Take a look," she said.

I turned and looked in the mirror. I didn't recognise myself. "Shit," I said, stunned. "You have to show me how to do that before we go home on Sunday."

"Happily," she said. "Now let's go and show you off to your man."

I stood up, and we walked out into the corridor. Rich and my boyfriend were waiting in his doorway for us.

Jane wandered over to Rich, who kissed and led her toward the exit. My boyfriend looked at me, and looked at me, and looked at me, then smiled.

"You like?" I said sweetly.

"Can we skip the night out, and I take you straight to bed?" he asked, half serious.

"As tempting as that is, and it really is, I haven't gone to all this trouble to stay in. I was hoping you might want to show me off?"

"Oh, that I really can do," he said, helping me put my coat on and taking my hand, leading me to the exit to catch up with the others. "But we're going to fuck all night when we get back," he whispered.

"I'll hold you to that," I replied.

Hours later, after a lot of dancing and alcohol, the large group we were part of started to disband, with some heading on to a club after the gig and some just disappearing inexplicably. Rich and Jane decided to head off to a club for a while, leaving me and my boyfriend with only one thing on our minds.

We left the student union and returned to his room quickly, his corridor empty as everyone else had carried on their evening. When we walked into his room, I was horny and ready and willing to have as much sex as we could handle.

He was on me as soon as we were in his room, and the door was closed. My coat was ripped off, and he pressed me against the back of the door, kissing me roughly.

"You looked so fucking hot tonight. Everyone wanted you," he said between kisses.

"If this is what it results in, I'll dress like this every day you're around," I said breathlessly as he ran his hands over my body and peeled my dress upwards and over my head.

I sat on the bed and took off my bra, boots, and tights. When I looked up, he had undressed quickly and stood before me naked.

"Bring that here and put it in my mouth," I said, gesturing to his cock. He stepped forward as I opened my mouth and guided his semi-rigid cock into my willing and eager mouth. I dearly loved sucking his cock and had missed it since he left for university. I lavished attention on it, licking every inch and sucking happily, moaning softly as I slid my face up and down on his growing shaft. If he hadn't stopped me, I'd have finished him right then, but thankfully he'd missed my body just as much as I'd missed his. He pressed me back onto the bed and climbed on top of me, kissing my neck and sliding down my body, kissing my chest, nipples and stomach, before eventually arriving at the top of my underwear. He wasted no time in removing it and casting it to one side. I opened my legs and saw him looking lovingly at my pussy, as if delighted to see an old friend.

He reached up and put a finger on my clit, and slowly slid it downward as I wriggled happily. He leaned forward, and I could feel his warm breath on my clit. I waited, but not for long. Seconds later, his tongue was all over my pussy. I was so happy to have him there again that I could've cried, but instead, I just moaned as he worked on me for a while until our collective desire for him to be inside me overwhelmed us.

6

"Fuck me?" I asked sweetly, running my hands through his hair as he lapped eagerly at my clit.

He didn't answer. He kissed my clit one final time and raised his body over mine. I pulled my legs back and held them open with my hands as he guided his cock into me and, without ceremony, took me in a way he had never before. It was as if he wanted to reclaim my body as his, fucking me aggressively, roughly, but not too much of either.

I responded. My desperation to feel him sliding his cock in and out of my young, tight pussy caused me to urge him on. With each impact of his pelvis against mine, I moaned louder and louder, my body eagerly welcoming his entire length into me.

He had stamina. I guess all men do at that age. He could go on and on, which always meant that sex was an activity we could do for hours, and sometimes we did. We were both more eager on this night, having had to wait so long, knowing we had all weekend for more. He prided himself on making me come in multiple positions before he came inside me himself. You can imagine — a girl loves that. It wasn't long before my moans turned to soft screams as he helped press my legs open and stared into my eyes as he drove into me, watching me head closer and closer to my first of the evening. I closed my eyes and started to scream as his relentless pursuit of my release pushed me to the edge, then right over it. My legs began to shake as he continued.

"I'm coming, oh god, I'm fucking coming," I muttered. Stating the obvious as my body shook beneath him. He continued pounding into me, maintaining my orgasm for quite a while, leaving me quivering and moaning beneath him as he slowed to let me pull myself together a little.

"Need a break?" he asked.

"No. I need more," I panted.

He withdrew, and I was over into my favourite position in a split second, on my hands and knees, my rear inviting him in. He traced a finger around my wet, inviting opening, then grabbed my hips and entered my body again. I moaned as he slid in deep, his body pounding again against my ass as he drove into my pussy. My first orgasm hadn't completely subsided, so it didn't take long for my toes to curl and my second — possibly a re-emergence of my first — built quickly. Again, he continued until I started to moan loudly and upped his pace to finish me, still refraining from finishing himself.

By this stage, I was a hot mess but still very horny and unwilling for the sex to end. As he was slowly fucking me, waiting for my second orgasmic high to subside, it turned and looked over my shoulder a little.

"Is this a full-service fuck?" I asked.

"What?"

"I want you to fuck my ass," I whispered. "But I'm worried I'll make too much noise."

He withdrew from inside me and reached for a little bottle of lube from his bedside drawer.

"Everyone's out. And besides, even if they weren't, I think it's a little late for you to worry about making noise," he laughed, moving back behind me.

I felt some of the cold lube on my rear opening, then him massaging it around with his finger and inserting it into me to make sure I was ready. He didn't know, and I never confessed, that I was more than ready, as the dildo I had at home to keep me company while he was at Uni had a habit of getting everywhere. It had been everywhere just last night.

I heard him pump the lube once more as I put my head down on the pillow, waiting for him. He worked the lube along his cock, then pressed his tip against my rear. I instantly relaxed and let him in. He stopped, shallow, to give me time to adjust to him in my back passage. I was in no mood for him to be gentle, so I closed my eyes and slid my body back, letting him watch as his cock disappeared inside me again.

"Now fuck me again, and don't stop until you've come," I begged.

8

"What? I never come in your..." he started.

"You do tonight," I insisted.

I knew he wanted to, and I'd never actually asked him not to, but at no point in the past during anal sex had he finished inside me. It seemed that my suggesting that he do so was all the inspiration he needed.

I spread my legs a little, lowering my pelvis slightly, allowing him to drive downward into me, and he wasted no time. It was only a moment before he gave my ass the same energy and attention he'd given my pussy a few moments ago. He put his hands on my shoulders, pulling my slim body back onto him as he thrust into me.

"You sure I can come in here," he asked.

"Very sure," I panted. "I want you to."

He groaned as he prepared to deposit his load inside my body. My body heated back up quickly, and I started to scream a little, mixed with vocal encouragement, which did the trick. I was quickly rewarded with another birthday present.

He lifted my body off the bed as he drove aggressively into me a few more times, and then he released what seemed like endless streams of his come into my rear. I came too, but given how animated he was, he may not have noticed.

After we'd finished, he withdrew, and I flopped down onto the bed to recover, satisfied.

We lay and cuddled naked for a while until, eventually, my boyfriend got up and went to make us a coffee in the shared kitchen. As he left the room, I could hear voices in the corridor as people returned from their Friday evening out. I lay there smiling at the ceiling, and the door opened. I looked over, expecting to see him with two coffees. Instead, I saw Jane peer through the door.

"Are you decent?" she asked.

"Yep," I replied from under the bed covers.

"Good night?" she asked. I smiled at her.

"We thought so."

"What?" I asked, curious.

"Rich and I and a few others have been back a while. We've been in the kitchen chatting. It sounded like you were having a lot of fun."

I was embarrassed, really embarrassed. My face started to go red.

"Don't worry. You're not the first girl who's screamed so loudly it's echoed down the corridors. I've done it, too," she said happily.

I relaxed a little.

"Mind if me and Rich join you when the men have made our coffees for a bit?" she asked.

"Not at all," I replied.

"Cool, I'll go and get out of this dress, and more importantly, these heels, and put something comfortable on," and she disappeared next door.

I needed to go to the toilet, so I stood, slipped my dress back over my naked body, and strolled into the corridor. I'd forgotten I had to pass the kitchen to get to the bathroom. With no tights or underwear on, my dress didn't leave much to the imagination. As I passed the door, I glanced in. There were about ten people in there, including my boyfriend and Rich, mostly male.

My boyfriend looked across to see me in my dress, hair ruffled, with almost the entire length of my legs on show. This was another new sight for him, and judging by the look in his eyes, a very welcome one. I was sure some others were quite happy at the view too, and I felt rather empowered.

I smiled at the group of guys looking at me and quickly went to the bathroom. After I returned, passing the kitchen slowly again to get a few more glances, I slipped into the new nightie he had bought me for my birthday. Ironically was longer than my dress, and I sat on the bed as he and Rich returned with four coffees. A few moments later, Jane arrived in a beautiful white silk nightie. She closed the door before sitting on the bed with me, opposite Rich, and my boyfriend, sitting on the little sofa.

We chatted briefly about the evening and what people had been up to, and then the conversation moved on to relationships. I was honest about my boyfriend being my first real relationship and my "first" sexually. It was easy to talk, as Rich and Jane were relative strangers who were very open and didn't judge at all. We laughed at me buying a really short dress to show off my legs and then wearing opaque tights as I couldn't bring myself to do it. Rich commented on how good I would have looked, given his brief glimpse of it on my way to the bathroom.

By this point, it was the early hours, and the alcohol had worn off, though nobody seemed particularly tired. Eventually, Jane lay on the bed and encouraged me to lie down next to her as we talked to our men, both of us making eyes at our respective other halves, anticipating more sex when we went our separate ways later.

As we were chatting, Jane moved onto her side next to me. I couldn't put my finger on it, but her being there was having an effect on me I hadn't expected. It was nice. It felt sexy.

"You two look ready for bed. Maybe we should leave them to it," Rich laughed, nodding to my boyfriend.

"I'd wanna stay and watch," my boyfriend said, smiling.

"Watch what?" Jane said seductively, putting one of her legs across mine momentarily.

My boyfriend smiled.

"Watch you two get naked together," Rich said.

I shuddered for a second, but not in disapproval. The thought felt sexy.

Jane looked at me, then whispered in my ear. "Mind if I kiss you, just for fun?"

My heart started beating hard, but the idea was a good one. I blinked in approval.

"It would look something like this," Jane said to them, then looked into my eyes and smiled. She leaned forward and put her hand behind my head, pulling me in, and kissed me deeply. The kiss lasted a while, and we enjoyed it a lot. I vaguely heard one of our boyfriends say, "Fucking hell", but I was so busy then that I'm not sure which one of them it was.

Eventually, Jane leaned back and ended the kiss. She smiled at me. "Fucking hell, P, maybe they should leave us to it," she said dreamily. This wasn't how I imagined this weekend would go.

"Sorry, there's no fucking way we're leaving now," my boyfriend said.

I glanced at him, trying to read him. His face told me everything I needed to know. He was into this.

I was into this.

Jane was into this.

Rich was into this.

The problem was I had no idea what to do next.

Jane, on the other hand, did. She lifted an arm and slowly drew her finger down my neck, across my collarbone, then over my nightie and down my body, switching to one side and caressing my leg. Driven by instinct, I bent the knee of the leg she was touching and raised it. My nightie lifted slightly, exposing a little of my smooth-shaven clit to the audience as I lay on my back. I didn't notice, but Jane did.

She slid her hand quickly up my leg to cover my modesty. "That's too pretty for all the world to see," she said, smiling. She left her hand there, her fingers achingly close to my clit. I could tell she was waiting for a reaction, and I completely forgot our boyfriends were watching just a few feet away as I felt my body reacting to her. Responding so positively, I blinked nervously and bit my bottom lip.

Jane lowered one finger onto my clit, and I shuddered with pleasure. Then she lowered another and gently pressed against my lowered leg. I instinctively bent the knee and shifted it away, giving her more access. She took advantage of the freedom and gently explored my clit further, my back arching as I whimpered at her touch.

I glanced across at our boyfriends, sitting silently, enjoying the show. Mine smiled and nodded a little, clearly happy with the situation. Jane slid her fingers to my opening, regaining my attention as she slid them inside me. I whimpered again.

"Seems she likes you, J," Rich said to her.

"Seems I like her too," she replied. I looked at her, and she smiled, then leaned in to kiss me again as she fingered me slowly, withdrawing occasionally to massage my clit. Eventually, the kissing stopped, but the attention she was giving my pussy didn't. She leaned forward and whispered again; "Do you mind if I taste you?" she asked.

I didn't reply. I just bent my outward knee further and let it fall away, exposing myself fully. She smiled.

"And this?" she asked, tugging gently at the hem of my nightie.

I glanced nervously at my boyfriend for his approval. He nodded. I lifted my bottom, and she pulled it up and over my head, then pressed my back down and kissed my chest, working one nipple at a time. By this point, I'd forgotten her boyfriend, a guy I'd met only hours ago, was watching too. Jane slid down my naked body, kissed my tummy, and slowly licked my groin. I was aching to feel her tongue on my clit. I closed my eyes and grasped my chest as she slid her tongue downward. As it touched my clit I moaned.

"Oh, fuck Jane."

I put my hand into her long wavy brown hair and pulled her in deeper. She worked my clit for a while, then giggled at me.

"You taste amazing," she said softly. "I think I need to explore more." She pressed my legs open further and buried her tongue in my, by now soaking wet pussy. We both moaned.

She continued for a little while, then sat up on her knees between my legs. She peeled off her nightie, dropped it on top of mine, and sat there, naked and beautiful.

"Wanna try?" she said seductively.

I'd stopped worrying about the boyfriends altogether at this stage and nodded. Jane pulled me down the bed a little, climbing over me in a sixty-nine and lowering her pussy toward my face slowly as she buried her tongue back into mine.

I'd never seen one this close before. I was studying it, trying to work out what I was going to do until I felt her go back to work on mine. Then I stopped thinking and just started doing, sliding my tongue across her clit. She moaned and lowered herself further. I took that as a good sign and set to work, trying desperately to concentrate on pleasing her while she flashed her tongue across my clit and into my pussy.

We lay there for a while, lost in each other's bodies, exploring every inch of each other's honeypots eagerly, moaning loudly, encouraging each other as our boyfriends watched.

Eventually, she slowed and lifted off me, sitting next to my head as she ran her fingers over my sex. I lay on my back, eyes closed, legs open, and moaning as Rich and my boyfriend studied my body.

"I think she's ready to fuck. Would one of you boy's mind?" she asked.

I opened my eyes, startled. My boyfriend would have been welcome inside me. He always was, but what she was suggesting was that she didn't mind which of them fucked me as long as one of them did. The thought of feeling a different cock inside me, only my second ever, was an instant thrill. But I wasn't about to risk my relationship for it.

I looked across at them, considering choosing on their behalf. Still, I stayed silent, curious to see what my boyfriend would say.

"I think Rich should fuck her. If she wants him to?" my boyfriend asked, smiling at me. Happy to let me choose without fear of consequences.

"So, whose cock do you fancy? Wanna try mine or stick with yours?"

"Yours," I whispered nervously.

She looked into my eyes and held my gaze as she spoke. "Rich, mind fucking this beautiful pussy for me?"

"My pleasure," he said, standing up and taking off his clothes as we watched. His cock was already rock hard when he freed it from his underwear. Hardly surprising, given he'd been watching me and his girlfriend having sex for the last half hour.

"Bring that here. I want to suck it first," Jane said casually. He walked around to the side of the bed where she was kneeling beside me and stood beside her as she eagerly took him in her mouth as I watched from below. She eventually looked down at me.

"Wanna suck my boyfriend's cock before we fuck you?" she asked.

I did, and at this stage, having had the green light from my watching boyfriend, I didn't refer for approval. Instead, I sat up as Rich offered his cock to me. I slid him into my mouth and worked him. He groaned happily. I was getting quite into it when Jane stopped us.

"I think it's time we fuck you," she said.

Rich withdrew his cock from my mouth, and butterflies filled my stomach as I lay back, and he climbed onto the bed between my already open legs.

I looked up at him. "Ready?" he whispered. I nodded nervously, then almost immediately felt the tip of his cock against my opening. I closed my eyes, and he entered me.

"Oh fuck," I moaned as only the second cock I'd ever experienced slid into my body. It felt different, good, but different. A little bigger, maybe. I felt full.

"She's tight," I heard him whisper. "Feels great."

"Doesn't she?" I heard my boyfriend agree happily, which just spurred me on. I lifted my legs and warped them around Rich as he got into a rhythm, sliding his cock inside me to the hilt with every thrust. I started to moan loudly, very loudly.

Jane, keen to be a part of the action, lifted her leg over my head and lowered her pussy towards my face once more. I lifted my head, desperately working her tongue while her boyfriend fucked me endlessly. I saw her lean forward and kiss him while she sat on my face, which caused him to move quicker, harder. I wasn't going to last king, and I knew it.

Jane sat back upright and held her pussy over my mouth while she started to work her clit with her fingers. She was heading to orgasm too, and I helped, sliding my tongue as deep into her as I could.

"Harder," she whispered to Rich.

He upped his pace, and Jane reached forward with her other hand and played with my clit while he pounded into me. I screamed a muffled scream.

"Are you going to come, P?" she asked.

I squeezed her leg, unable to respond with my tongue deep in her pussy.

"Good, so are we," she panted.

She came first, shuddering above me and grinding herself down onto my face as she came. I loved it and continued lapping up her juices.

The sight of Jane coming on my face made Rich groan, and she worked my clit harder. Just as my legs started to shake violently around his body, he slammed into me and unloaded inside me hard.

Jane slid off and sat beside me again as he slowed. She was panting herself and watching as he finished depositing his come in my body. He slid out.

"Allow me," she said. And he stood again as she cleaned his and my juices off his glistening cock with her mouth.

He dressed, sat back down as Jane lay next to me, and stroked my body slowly while we caught our breath.

"We should probably get to bed," she said. "After that, I have a feeling your boyfriend will want to fuck you too."

I looked across at him, and his eyes were glistening. Jane was right.

She stood up and slipped her nightie back on.

"Come on, let's leave them to it," she said, holding her hand out to Rich. As they reached the door, she turned.

"You're amazing, P," she said. "Mind if we borrow her again sometime if she wants to?" she asked my boyfriend.

"If she wants to," he replied.

They all looked at me. I just smiled sheepishly and bit my bottom lip.

"I'll take that as a yes," Jane said. "Goodnight both, see you tomorrow.

They left quickly and closed the door. I turned to look at my boyfriend.

"You didn't seem surprised?" I said.

I knew Jane was bi, and they had a few threesomes with women. She told me she wanted you this afternoon."

"Why didn't you tell me?" I asked curiously.

"I thought it better for you to make your own choices in the moment rather than anticipate them and be nervous."

"Clever," I said approvingly.

"So, was she right? Do you wanna fuck now they have gone?" I asked seductively, hoping she was.

"Yeah, I was hoping to come in that beautiful ass of yours again," he said, standing up and walking toward the bed.

I smiled. He took off his clothes quickly, and I lifted my legs, threading them behind my arms, my come-filled pussy on display to him as he prepared to fuck my ass.

"Fuck me like this. I want to see your face when you come in me."

He smiled. "Where's this come from?"

"Maybe visiting you at uni is opening my eyes a little," I said, becoming excited as he lubed his cock and climbed onto the bed.

"And your legs, it seems," he said.

"Is that a bad thing?" I asked, then moaned as he slid his cock into my rear.

17

"Does it look like a bad thing?" he asked, pressing his entire length into my back passage for the second time today.

I smiled up at him blissfully, and he leaned down and kissed me, holding still inside me. He leaned back a little.

"I think we could be good friends with Jane and Rich," he said.

"Me too," I agreed, as he pulled out to his tip and started to fuck me roughly again.

November 2007 – A stranger, a sequin dress, and a foursome

A few weeks after my first threesome with my boyfriend's neighbour and his girlfriend, it was time for me to visit him at university again. I was disappointed that his neighbour's girlfriend, Jane, couldn't make it that weekend. I loved having sex with her and Rich while my boyfriend watched, and the sex my boyfriend and I had afterwards was even more explosive than usual.

In any case, I was madly in love and couldn't wait to see him again. Having picked up a few tips from Jane and finally realised that my long slim legs were an asset, I had ordered some short skirts and dresses for casual wear, which I'd never done before, usually preferring leggings or jeans.

I packed up my new clothes, including a sexy little number to wear out to a club on Saturday night and some lingerie. I excitedly jumped on the train on Saturday lunchtime in a little summer dress.

It was a few hours on the train, and despite my newfound confidence to expose a little flesh, I was still a little paranoid. Not for long, though. I quickly noticed that many guys of various ages had given me glances as they passed or sat in nearby seats. Just the glances themselves improved my confidence – and curiously, they turned me on. There was one guy – I'd say in his mid-twenties, at least six or seven years older than me at the time, and very attractive. He sat at my table opposite me. He was reading a book, but each time I looked at him, he looked at me. We kept exchanging glances, and I felt guilty, so I decided to distract myself. I sent a selfie I took before I left to my boyfriend.

'Fuck, you look hot. Can't wait to get under that later.'

I smiled to myself and bit my bottom lip.

'You're not the only one that wants to get under it, it seems', I replied.

'Oh?' he asked.

I replied and told him about the stranger sitting opposite that kept looking at me. I was vague about how good-looking he was.

'Can't say I blame him. If I was sitting on that train with you, I'd wanna fuck you too. Is he good-looking?'

I wouldn't lie.

'Yes.'

'Is he turning you on?'

'Yes.'

There was a pause in the messages for a moment. I glanced up. He was looking again. He smiled. I smiled back. My phone rang, and I answered it through my headphones.

"P, it's Jane. I'm with Rich and your boyfriend."

"Jane? I didn't think you were coming this weekend?"

"Change of plan. I'm here. We're waiting for you to get here. Listen, we're all horny at the thought of you fucking a stranger on a train. What do you think?"

"All?"

"All, your boyfriend started it."

"Really?"

"Yeah,"

"Jane, you know I've only...."

"Fucked him, Rich, and me, yeah, I know. Fancy adding another one?"

I looked up at him. He was hot.

"On a train? How?"

"Pass him the phone."

"What?"

"Pass him the phone."

I unplugged my headphones and passed the phone to him.

"My friend wants to speak to you," I said nervously.

He took my phone and held it to his ear. I couldn't hear what Jane said to him, just what he said in reply and his body language.

"Hello?

"Hello, Jane."

"Yes."

"Erm, yes," – he glances at me.

"Yes, I have."

"Not many, almost empty."

"Uh-huh."

"Okay."

He shook his head in shock a little and passed me the phone. "She wants to talk to you."

"Hello?" I said, not bothering with my headphones.

"After the next stop, go to the toilet, but don't lock it. Take your phone. He has condoms with him. He's going to fuck you."

My heart started to beat in my chest, and I looked up to see him rifling in his bag as he slipped a condom wrapper into his jeans pocket.

"Erm, okay," I said, equally horny and nervous.

"Ring us afterwards and tell us how it went. He'll move to another seat after you're done."

He closed his book and put it on the table as the train pulled into the next station. He glanced across at me and smiled. Suddenly my nerves vanished, and I was a horny mess, waiting for the train to leave. My phone vibrated.

'You're making me so horny. I'm tearing that dress off you later.' My boyfriend wrote.

Between the atmosphere, the anticipation, and the message, I could feel my body getting warmer in a nice tingly way. I loved that my boyfriend was into this – as surreal as it was.

The doors closed, and it seemed like an age before the train slowly started to edge away. I slipped my phone into the pocket of my dress, shuffled from my seat, stood in the aisle for a second, and then walked down the carriage to the toilet. I pressed the button, and the large door swung open. I glanced across to see him getting out of his seat. I stepped in and pressed the button to close the door but didn't lock it. Seconds later, as I stood leaning against a handrail, the door opened, and he stepped in, quickly closing it behind him and pressing the lock button.

He turned to look at me, a little nervous.

Usually, I'm the nervous one in any situation, but I was so horny I stepped forward and then looked up into his eyes.

"We don't have much time," I whispered, reaching for the button on his jeans. He got on board quickly and pulled the condom wrapper from his pocket before helping to unbutton them. I slid them and his underwear down and looked at his cock, which wasn't yet fully ready to penetrate me. I bent over and was about to take it in my mouth when he spoke.

"I've been told to take photos on your phone for evidence. Jane insisted."

I unlocked my phone, passed it to him, and knelt again as he leaned back against the wall. I took him in my mouth as I looked into the camera. He moaned at my eagerness. I sucked his cock until it was hard enough to put on the condom, then stood up as he quickly rolled it into place. By this point, he had found his groove, and he turned me around and had me bend over, holding on to the rail to keep me steady. He lifted my dress over my ass and knelt behind me, taking more photos as he pulled my panties down while feeling my long legs at the same time. He kissed my pussy, flicked his tongue over my opening, then stood up and guided his cock into my wetness. I moaned loudly as only the third cock I had ever experienced stretched my pussy walls apart and took up residence inside me.

He gave me a second or two to adjust to his size, then took hold of one of my hips and started to fuck me quickly, taking photos on my camera with his spare hand.

I'd never really had a 'quickie' before. I didn't get the point. But now I got it. The physical sensation, the raw energy, the desperation to enjoy a quick fuck. I was so horny and probably a little too loud, but he fucked me like he meant it, and I fed off his energy. I loved the rawness of the whole thing, a stranger taking me in a public toilet and photographing it for my boyfriend and his friends. He eventually put my phone down on a shelf and grabbed my other hip as he bought himself to orgasm, pounding into me as he finished. He slowed a little, then withdrew to deal with the full condom.

I pulled up my panties and slipped my phone back into my pocket as he dressed himself.

We looked at each other. I followed my instinct and leaned forward and kissed his cheek.

"Thanks, that was amazing," I whispered.

"No, thank you, you're beautiful, by the way," he said sweetly. I blushed. "Wait here and count to twenty, then go back to your seat, okay?" he said.

"Okay,"

"It was lovely to meet you," he said, reaching for the button.

"Fuck me, you mean?" I said seductively.

He turned as the door opened, and I stood behind it.

"Both." He said as I closed and locked the door behind him.

I counted to twenty, opened the door, and returned to my seat. He was gone.

I sat and flicked through the photos of my slutty liaison. Given I hadn't had an orgasm while we were fucking, I was still horny, really horny. The photos didn't help. I texted my boyfriend.

'Back at my seat.'

'How was it?'

'Hot'

'Show us.'

23

I sent a photograph of me staring into the camera with his cock in my mouth, then a few of his cock disappearing inside me from behind.

'Fucking hell! Put your headphones in. Jane is going to call.'

A moment later, my phone rang.

"Hey slut," Jane said. "That looked fun. Warmed up for some fun with us later?"

"God, yes," I replied.

"Good, we're all looking forward to seeing you again. Get here soon!"

I was sitting on a train in a short dress, horny as hell, my pussy slowly soaking my panties at the promise of more debauchery at the university that evening. A passer-by would have noticed something was up. Still, I tried to compose myself and counted the stops until I arrived at my destination. When I did, there he was, my boyfriend, standing with a coffee and a rose, waiting patiently for me.

I stepped off the train and threw myself at him, kissing him deeply before he picked up my bag and guided me to a waiting bus. We didn't mention my liaison on the train again, ever. However, he repeatedly caressed my exposed legs, clearly impressed with my new look. When we arrived at his room, Jane and Rich popped in to say hi.

Jane came over and put an arm around me affectionately.

"We're getting dressed early and going into the city for dinner. The boys are treating us before we hit the club, okay?"

"Okay, I said happily. Are we changing together again?"

"Yep, grab your stuff and come with me. The boys are getting ready in here."

We went into Rich's room to dress, and I pulled out my dress for the evening from my bag and laid it on the bed.

"That's nice," Jane said, looking at it in the mirror while doing her make-up.

"Thanks. What are you wearing?" I asked.

"Red sequins in the wardrobe."

I opened Rich's wardrobe, and there it was. A scandalously short, halter-neck, red sequin dress. There was nothing to it.

"Wow, Jane, that's amazing," I said, jealous of the dress and her confidence to wear it.

"You should get one; it would look amazing with your legs."

"I don't think I'd have the nerve to wear something like that in public," I said honestly.

"You fucked a stranger in a public toilet this afternoon, honey."

"Yeah, but the door was closed!" I protested.

"Try it on," she said casually.

"Really?"

"Yeah, why not? There's only us here. You can get a feel for it."

I couldn't resist. I removed my dress and bra and slipped into it as Jane tied the halter neck for me. I felt naked.

"You need to look in the mirror," Jane said, pointing at the full-length mirror inside Rich's wardrobe door. "No, wait," she said, rooting in my bag and pulling out my little black high-heeled suede boots. "These first."

I put them on, then stood up and looked in the mirror.

To say that I was impressed would be a massive understatement. My legs did look amazing, propped up on heels with a dress so short that my ass was almost showing, and my hair flowing down my exposed back just finished the look perfectly. I sighed happily.

"Beautiful," Jane said.

I glowed. "I want one."

Jane laughed and pulled an almost identical black sequin dress from the wardrobe.

"What's that?" I asked.

"My dress for the evening," she said.

"What?"

"That's yours. This is mine."

"What?"

"Your boyfriend treated you. I just did the shopping."

"What?"

"Fucking hell, P. Get with it."

I looked in the mirror again.

"But..."

"Wear that tonight, and I have a feeling you'll have a night you will never forget. We have half an hour, and you need to do your make-up and all that hair, come on."

I sat happily in my chair as Jane did my make-up. Yet again, she went all sultry and smoky. I straightened my long brown hair and put it in a ponytail, then stood in front of the mirror. I wasn't sure I recognised myself, but I liked who I saw, nonetheless.

"Oooh missed something," Jane said.

"What?"

Jane rifled in her bag and pulled out a new black lace thong.

"You can't wear full panties in that. It defeats the purpose," she said, passing it to me.

I knew she was right, but I was still a little nervous at the thought. I slipped out of my existing underwear and into the thong.

Jane stood with me and took a selfie.

"We're going to get so laid tonight," she said excitedly.

We stepped out of Rich's room onto the corridor to see him and my boyfriend dressed in a shirt and jeans, chatting with a group of the other guys that lived on their floor. Every one of them stopped and looked at us. Jane stepped behind me and squeezed my ass.

"Off you go," she whispered, encouraging me forward.

I breathed in, and my heels clicked as I sauntered toward my boyfriend. His eyes were glistening at the sight of me. I became confident, foxy even, wiggling my hips gently as I approached him.

Jane watched, like a proud parent, then joined us.

"Hot, isn't she?" she said to everyone in the corridor.

Lots of the guys nodded, adding to my confidence, though I pretended to blush a little.

We headed out to dinner in a taxi and arrived at a nice restaurant inside a swanky hotel in the city. As we walked from the taxi to the restaurant, I noticed more admiring glances in our direction. That said, Jane and I did look hot, and together we were even hotter.

We ate our dinner and drank quite a lot, with me sitting opposite Rich and Jane opposite my boyfriend. I found out that evening that Jane was from a wealthy family and had bought my dress, but she didn't think I'd accept it unless I thought it was a present from my boyfriend.

At about ten in the evening, having sat drinking cocktails after dinner for some time, the waiter came over with the bill.

"Put it on suite nineteen," she said, signing for it.

Everyone looked at me and smiled.

"What?" I asked. "Whose staying in suite nineteen?"

"We are?"

"You and Rich?"

"Nope, all of us," Jane said.

"Are we going clubbing?" I asked naively.

"No, sweetheart, we're not," Jane said, looking at Rich and my boyfriend.

"I'm confused," I said, looking at my boyfriend. He smiled, reached across the table, and took my hand.

"Jane has organised a bit of a treat for us all," he said.

"Daddy paid for it," she said.

"So, we're not going clubbing?" I asked again.

"No, there's music, alcohol, and privacy upstairs, sweetie. And we don't get our shoes vomited on or groped by a guy with bad breath that needs a shower."

It dawned on me. This was another night of debauchery with the three of them—only this time, without the tiny bed and the audience in the adjacent rooms. I smiled and bit my bottom lip.

"We should probably go upstairs then, don't you think?" I said.

The three of them smiled, and we all stood up and headed to the elevator.

Moments later, we were inside a vast two-bedroomed suite near the top of the hotel, with a lounge, a balcony, and a bar. Jane put on some music, then came and grabbed my hand and shouted to our boyfriends to make drinks while we were gone. She dragged me to one of the bathrooms and closed the door.

"You could have warned me," I said happily.

"We thought it would be fun not to," she said, touching up her lipstick in the mirror.

"Anyway, this could get messy, so I wanted to talk boundaries before we drink any more alcohol," she said, putting her lipstick away and her hands on my hips.

"Okay," I said nervously.

"So?"

"I don't know. I mean, the last time we were together, you and Rich fucked me in front of my boyfriend. I'm not sure I have any boundaries."

Jane laughed. "So, is anything off the table?"

"Kissing Rich. You, yes. My boyfriend, yes. Rich, no."

"Okay, we're getting somewhere."

"Can your boyfriend fuck me?"

"Well, yours fucked me, so it would only be fair if he could," I said, nervously but growing hornier by the second. "But you can't kiss him," I added quickly.

"Done, any more boundaries?" she asked.

"No."

"Wait, you did say I could kiss you, didn't you?"

"Yes," I said, my heart starting to beat faster.

"Good," she said, turning my back to the worktop with her hands still on my hips and pressing me against it with her body. I closed

28

my eyes and tilted my head, and she kissed me deeply. She slid her hands around me onto my bare back, gently stroked my shoulders, and stepped back.

"I think we're overdressed," she said.

"What? We're practically naked as it is, have been all night."

She slid her hands back to my hips and down to the bottom of my dress, lifting it and hooking her thumbs over the waistband of my thong.

"You won't need this," she said, kneeling slowly and dragging it down my legs to the floor. She looked at my pussy while she was kneeling in front of me, then leaned forward and kissed my clit softly. She knew how to turn me on. She stood back up and turned her back to me, then slowly removed her thong, bending at the waist as her ass slid out the back of her dress and her pussy came into sight. I reached forward and slid my finger up her opening. She dropped her thong and held onto her ankles like a gymnast, holding her body in position. I couldn't resist her, so I knelt and slid my tongue inside her. She tasted exactly as I had remembered her from our last (and so far, only) night of passion. Perfect. She moaned softly as I explored her once more. The door knocked.

"Have you two got lost in there?" my boyfriend called.

"No, but give us a sec. P's got her tongue in my pussy, and I don't want her to stop yet." Jane panted.

He tried the door, and it wasn't locked. I heard it swing open as I carried on the task at hand, and they both saw us side on. Jane bent over, holding her ankles as I knelt behind her, stroking her legs as I lapped eagerly at her pussy. I carried on, letting them watch for a few moments, then went deep inside her with my tongue one last time before withdrawing and kissing her opening one last time. Then we both stood up and held each other in front of them.

"Sorry, you two, but one of these weekends, I'm having a whole night alone with her. I smiled at her, and she kissed me briefly before we parted and went to our boyfriends. She and Rich went in front of us to the bar area, where the music was still playing. "You need to taste her," I told my boyfriend, indicating I was happy for him to be with her.

"I will, but first, I want to taste you."

Rich passed cocktails to Jane and me and a beer to my boyfriend, taking one himself.

"All these cocktails. Anybody would think you two needed to get us drunk to take advantage of us," Jane said, giggling a little. "You do know we'd fuck you both sober," she added. "Anyway, before I drink this, P and I have agreed," she said. "Anybody can do whatever the fuck they want with whoever the fuck they want, as long as you boys only kiss your girlfriends. Okay?"

Our boyfriends nodded.

"Fuck, we didn't talk condoms," she blurted out.

"Well, I've had sex with them both without one already, so I'm not going to start now," I said – listening to myself speaking but not believing I said it.

"Do you want him to use one with me?" she asked, nodding at my boyfriend, who looked a little uncomfortable being the subject of a conversation he wasn't included in.

"No, do you?"

"God, no. Fab, that's settled then," she said.

Jane turned the music up, then wandered to the balcony to look over the edge. Rich followed.

"Did you say you wanted to taste me?" I asked, turning to my boyfriend, horny and desperate for some of his attention. He put down his bottle and lifted me onto the bar, then knelt before me as I lifted a leg onto one of the stools. "No underwear?" he asked.

"Seemed pointless," I said, sipping my cocktail happily as he leaned forward and kissed my clit, just as Jane had done, then started eagerly working it with his tongue. I was in heaven, moaning and running my fingers through his hair as Jane and Rich returned from the balcony and

30

stood watching him, pleasuring me. Jane came over, and Rich helped her onto the bar beside me. "Want to try mine?" she said softly, also lifting her leg onto a stool. My boyfriend looked up from between my legs and glanced at me. I nodded. He shuffled across as I watched, and he lapped at Jane's pussy for a second, then stopped and looked at me.

"You're right. She tastes amazing," he said, returning to work on Jane as she put her glass down and leaned back onto the bar top.

I looked at Rich and smiled. "I guess that leaves you with me." He smiled back and put down his bottle and knelt between my legs next to my boyfriend, and went to work on me. I leaned back onto the bar next to Jane.

"Did you say I taste amazing?" she panted as my boyfriend massaged her clit with his tongue.

"Yes, you do," I said. She put her hand behind my neck, pulled me closer and kissed me as Rich slid his fingers into my wetness, and my boyfriend did the same to her. We lay there for a while, greedily enjoying the attention of our lovers until Jane decided it was time to switch things up.

"Come on," she whispered, sitting up and pulling me up next to her. We slid off the bar and stood together. She reached behind me and tugged at the bow holding my halter neck in place. It fell, and rather than rushing to cover my breasts, I let it fall, wriggled the dress over my hips, and let it drop to the floor in front of all three of them. I stood there, naked but for my boots for a second, then reached up and tugged on Jane's bow, allowing her to do the same. We stood before our men naked for a second and then stepped forward. Jane to Rich, me to my boyfriend. We undid their shirts and removed them, then their jeans, then underwear, until they stood before us, naked and semi-hard.

"I'm just popping to the loo for a second. Mind looking after the boys on your own for a while?" Jane said.

"Not at all," I replied, kneeling and taking a cock in each hand as Jane sauntered away in her heels, finished a cocktail, and disappeared into the bathroom. I turned to my boyfriend first and licked the length of his cock while I slid my hand along Rich's shaft and played with his balls a little. I took my boyfriend in my mouth and devoured him eagerly, continuing to play with Rich's balls while I did so. I turned quickly, greedy to have them both to myself for a moment, and dipped my head to take Rich into my mouth while my boyfriend watched. Once they both stood to attention, I slid my mouth deep onto them, one at a time, alternating between them. I didn't hear Jane come back and sit on a bar stool watching. After a little while, she shouted to me.

"Hey, greedy girl. Mind if I take over?"

I slid Rich out of my mouth and stood, wiping my mouth and giggling as I wandered over to the bar to my cocktail, and she knelt between them, starting with my boyfriend.

I watched as she worked him. He loved it, I could tell; having sucked his cock hundreds of times in the past, I knew what he liked, and this, he liked. Watching my friend suck him turned me on, and Rich, who she moved to shortly afterwards, gagging a little as she went deep on them both. Eventually, she stood up.

"P and I are going to the bedroom," she said to them. Bring cocktails, and we'll let you do anything you want to us," she said seductively.

She wasn't wrong. By that point, I was up for anything, and I mean anything.

As we strolled into the bedroom together, she left the door open, and we lay on the bed together, kissing and caressing each other's bodies.

"I forgot to ask," she whispered. "What are your thoughts on anal?" I smiled.

"As you said, we'll let them do anything to us," I replied quietly.

They came in and went to either side of the bed. My boyfriend bought a cocktail and a beer over to the side I was nearer to, and Rich did the same on Jane's side. Jane and I carried on kissing as they spooned behind each of us. My boyfriend wasted no time sliding his cock into my pussy from behind. I gasped, delighted. A moment later, Jane gasped.

"Do you have a cock in you?" I asked.

"Yes," she panted. "You?"

"Yes," I sighed happily.

We tried to concentrate on kissing each other while our boyfriends fucked us from behind, but it was useless. We reluctantly let go of each other.

"Ride him," she said.

"Okay," I replied eagerly. My boyfriend heard her. He slid his cock out of me and lay on his back. I stood on the bed carefully, still in my heels, then squatted onto my knees as he guided his cock back into me. I rode his cock, moaning loudly as Jane and Rich watched while he continued to fuck her. A few moments later, Jane mounted Rich, and we sat beside each other, riding our boyfriends' cocks.

"Fancy swapping?" she asked.

I nodded, and we slipped off our boyfriends and switched. I slid Rich's cock inside me, and he stretched my pussy walls as I remembered from our last time. I breathed in deeply as I took all of him into me, then watched eagerly as my boyfriend's cock, my favourite cock, my cock, disappeared inside my friend's pussy, and she started to ride it. I nearly came just watching. I rode Rich's cock for a while but was a little distracted by what Jane was doing to my boyfriend beside me.

"Fancy a show?" she asked, pulling her hair from her body as she started to sweat.

"Yes," I replied.

"I'll need my boyfriend."

"Oh, I said, sliding off him and lying on the bed next to my boyfriend as she continued to ride him, and Rich got up.

"Do you really want to try this, babe?" Rich said.

"Fuck yes," she panted. Rich picked up a bottle of lube from the bedside table I'd not noticed and smeared it on his cock, then climbed between my boyfriend's legs and smeared some on Jane's ass.

I couldn't believe what I was seeing. I stayed silent, watching eagerly as Jane stilled herself on my boyfriend's cock and arched her pelvis forward. She reached down and took my hand.

"I have a feeling this might hurt, but I've been dying to try it," she said as Rich got into position. She stayed still as he pressed his cock against her rear.

"Relax, Jane, let him in," I encouraged. She took a deep breath and relaxed as his cock slid inside her rear slowly. She started to pant and moan loudly.

"Too much?" Rich asked.

"No," she insisted, adjusting.

After a moment, her breath steadied. She opened her eyes and let go of my hand.

"Fuck," she said softly. "This feels fucking amazing, fuck me, both of you."

My boyfriend started rocking his pelvis up and down, guiding his cock deep into her pussy, as Rich began to move in her ass, slowly at first, then getting faster. Jane howled and came quickly (and loudly) from the feeling of having two cocks inside her, screaming and shaking. Our men, however, did not. Not yet, at least. When she calmed a little, she looked down at me.

Rich withdrew carefully from her rear. He went to the bathroom to clean up the lube and returned as she climbed off my boyfriend.

"You have to try that," she said.

"Okay," I said eagerly, not thinking, just doing.

"Sit up. Let's try it differently," Jane said to my boyfriend, who bunched up the pillows and lay more upright.

"Allow me," she said, picking up the lube bottle and massaging it into my boyfriend's cock as I lay beside them, watching.

"Sit on it," she said softly.

I got up, crouched, facing away from him, and lay back onto his body, opening my legs wide. Jane gave me a cheeky smile, then massaged some lube into my ass, spending more time over it than simply to lubricate me. Then she guided his cock into my rear as I slowly slid down his body, still lying back onto him. I moaned as I felt him enter and closed my eyes.

I waited for Rich to fuck me, but he didn't, not immediately. Jane buried her tongue in my pussy while my boyfriend's cock was in my ass. I opened my eyes as she slid her tongue down, meeting my rear where his cock entered me, then down what was exposed of his shaft and licked his balls for a second.

"Sorry, got carried away," she said, sitting up. "Rich, would you mind?"

I held my legs up and open as my boyfriend took the weight of my body, lifting and lowering me slowly onto his cock while we waited for Rich to get into position, then stopped still as he entered me. I screamed. A lot. And I'm told I begged them to fuck me senseless. I don't remember, it's a blur, but I do know that having Rich pounding my pussy while my boyfriend fucked my ass sent me over the edge and left me there. When I came round, I was lying on the bed, being spooned by Jane. The boys had cleaned up and made more drinks, Jane had cleaned me up, and she was playing gently with my nipples, more for her enjoyment than mine.

"Hey there," she said, passing me a cocktail as I sat up.

"That was..." I started.

"Mind-blowing? I know, we have to do that again sometime."

I murmured my approval happily. I sat there, surrounded by naked bodies, as we all carried on drinking. Jane slid her hand up the inside of my leg, and I instinctively opened it further for her to tease my clit as we sat together.

"So, I've had an idea," she said softly.

I looked at her curiously.

"How about we 69...."

"Yes!" I exclaimed quickly, keen to taste her again.

"Wait!" she said, "I haven't finished."

"Sorry. Go."

"How about we 69, while Rich fucks you, and your boyfriend fucks me, then when they're done, we can clean our own boyfriends come out of each other."

"Still yes!" I exclaimed. We put down our glasses, and Jane lay down as I straddled her face and leaned down. My boyfriend came over to my face, semi-hard again from the break in the action, so I took him straight into my mouth and let him fuck it gently as he became hard again. As I didn't feel Jane's mouth on me, I imagine she did the same for Rich.

My boyfriend slid out of my mouth, and then I leaned forward, licking Jane's clit, feeling her body react, and then nodded to my boyfriend, who slid his cock into her. I heard Jane speak to Rich. "Let's make her come again." Then I felt a tongue on my clit as he slid his cock into me.

This worked. If it wasn't sexy enough that I was licking a sexy girl's clit, while I watched my boyfriend's cock slide into her, less than an inch from my face. I was also dealing with that girl licking my clit as her boyfriend fucked me. I wanted to come, but I wanted the men to come more, then when they did, Jane and I had each other to ourselves for a little while. Rich went to town on me. He'd fucked both Jane and me tonight, multiple times, but had not yet been able to finish., He earned it, and Jane's moans encouraged him as he fucked me. I moaned, too, and eventually, I felt him tense. I lifted my mouth off Jane's clit as Rich started to groan loudly and pound me deeper. I looked up at my boyfriend. "Fuck her, come in her, do it for me, baby," I said, panting at the fucking I was taking myself. He did as I asked and upped his pace dramatically, making Jane scream with pleasure under me. The guys came inside us a split second apart from each other, filling both our pussies with their sticky loads, with both of our encouragement. When they finished, they slowly withdrew and left us to it, heading back to the lounge.

"Mmmm," Jane said as I felt her lick some of Rich's load from within me. "Mind if I take my time?"

I looked down at my boyfriend's semen, which was starting to leak out of her. I licked it a little and swallowed it greedily.

"Well, we have all night," I said.

"Then we're staying in here together until they come in a fuck us again, agreed?" Jane said.

I kissed her clit gently.

"Agreed," I said, then cleaned her pussy slowly and erotically with my tongue as she did the same to me.

December 2007 – Two hot girls and a group of horny boys

My next trip to the university was planned to coincide with my boyfriend's birthday. I remember the call I made to him a few weeks before. I'll never forget it. I asked him what he wanted for his birthday, and of course, he mentioned random stuff, a console game, some aftershave, and stuff like that. Then, given my visits to him often resulted in me having my legs open most of the weekend, I asked him if there was anything he'd like to do for his birthday while I was there. He knew what I was asking. I half expected him to ask for another sexy night with his friend Rich and his girlfriend, Jane. But he and Rich had chatted and had other ideas.

Since my last visit when Jane and I went out practically naked in sequin backless mini dresses, much to the delight of everyone living in my boyfriend and Rich's corridor, there had been some conversation amongst them all. Fourteen guys lived on that corridor, and while some kept themselves to themselves, Rich and my boyfriend had become pretty good friends with quite a few of them. Most of which had said how hot Jane and I were. Boys being boys, it turns out that Rich and my boyfriend had told them all about how they had both fucked us both and all the sexy details. Bragging probably.

In any case, they'd had a proposition. Rich knew Jane would be into it, so he waited until I'd been asked before he mentioned it to her. The guys had suggested a 2-girl gangbang – all of them, and me and Jane. So, when I asked him what he'd like us to do for his birthday, he asked.

Can't blame a guy for trying, I guess. He didn't expect me to say yes.

The thing is, and looking back now, I probably made the decision too quickly. I was flattered. If you remember how all this started, when I met him, I was shy, hiding under baggy jumpers and didn't have the highest self-esteem or confidence. In the last nine months, I'd become confident, happy, and sexual. Very sexual.

So, I said I'd call Jane and if she said yes, I would be happy to.

I think he was shocked. And I know he was excited.

Well, it was for his birthday, after all...

So, I rang Jane and explained the situation. She jumped at it. Our boyfriends' friends weren't unattractive, and we all got on well enough. Jane and I had become comfortable enough to wander their corridor in skimpy nightwear, heading to and from the bathroom frequently when we went to visit.

I rang him back and said we were up for it, but not at the halls of residence. With Daddy's credit card again, Jane would book a suite at a hotel in town.

A plan emerged. Jane booked the room, and the guys were charged with getting alcohol and food sorted to take up to the suite for the evening – and numbers were agreed—six in total – including our boyfriends.

When I arrived at the station on the day, Jane met me at the station, and we went to the hotel – to be joined later by the guys.

She'd managed to get the same suite we had last time when we spent the evening fucking each other's boyfriends and each other. I was nervous but horny. Jane had a feeling I would be and had put a few bottles of prosecco on ice for us to drink while we got ready.

• • • •

When we arrived, we both stripped down to our underwear and put on hotel gowns while Jane opened the first bottle. We sat together on the sofa in the lounge, the sun streaming in through the windows.

"This is going to be so much fucking fun," Jane said excitedly.

"Have you ever done anything like this before?" I asked.

"Nope," she replied. "Rich and I have fucked other singles and couples together, but nothing on this scale. It's making me horny just thinking about it. Aren't you horny?"

"Maybe," I said, smiling from behind my prosecco glass. "But nervous too."

"Fuck that," she replied. "This is going to make their fucking year. According to Rich, some of those guys have been obsessing over us for a while. They will be putty in our hands, especially when they see us. Which reminds me, what are you wearing?"

"Just a black lace bra and thong," I replied. I didn't think we needed anything.

Jane laughed. "Babe, if you're going to be a porn star for the night, you must look like one. Luckily for you, I had a feeling you would say that, so I shopped for both of us."

"What?" I asked, confused.

"Come with me."

She took my arm, led me to the bedroom, and put her overnight case on the bed. She pulled out two basques, a black one with maroon details and a red one with black details.

"Red one's yours. You looked fucking hot in the red sequin dress," Jane said, returning to the case. She pulled out two pairs of fishnet stockings, again one in red and one in black, then two pairs of strappy high heels, red and black, then two very short satin robes – guess what? – one red and one black. Then she closed the case.

"No panties?" I asked.

"They came with the basques, but there's no point, besides you would have to wear them over the stocking straps to let the guys pull them off easily."

"I've never worn anything like this before," I said, nerves returning.

"With legs as long as yours, this will look seriously fucking hot. Besides, I'm here, and I've already planned your make-up."

"Really?"

"Yeah, I like doing your make-up, I can make you look as hot as I want to be, and tonight, I'm going to make us both look hot."

We returned to our drinks and finished the bottle, quickly moving to the next one. The alcohol, and Jane's excitement, helped my nerves. I knew that when everyone arrived, she would lead and make things easier for me. As the December sun set, we showered together and started getting ready with just over an hour to go until the guys arrived. Jane helped me into my basque and stockings, then I tied up my hair, and she did my make-up, careful not to let me see it until finished. She stepped away from the mirror, and I looked at myself, sitting in red lingerie, fishnet stockings, jet-black eyes, and cherry-red lips. I smiled, not recognising myself.

"You look hot," she said proudly.

"And easy," I added.

"You're not easy. You are in control of your sexuality and your body. None of that misogynistic bullshit about women who like sex being sluts. Fucking winds me up," she ranted.

She made a good point. I felt confident, sexy, and very horny.

"Go and look in the full-length mirror," she said. "Get the full effect."

I stood up, casually strolled to the mirror, and looked at myself.

"I saw that," she said.

"What?"

"Confidence. I've never seen you walk that confidently. Head up, shoulders back. Suits you."

I turned sideways and admired myself.

"I'd fuck you," Jane said. "Oh, wait, I have, and at some stage tonight, I'm sure I will again."

"Reckon we'll have the chance?"

"Are you kidding? We'll make the chance," she said.

I went to the lounge and refilled the glasses while Jane did her make-up, then we both put on our satin robes (which barely covered our asses), tidied the bedroom and went to the lounge. As we sat down, my phone pinged. It was my boyfriend.

'We're here, in the lobby. Last chance to change your mind – no pressure.'

"They're here," I said to Jane, still looking at my phone.

"Good," she said. "I'm ready, you?"

I breathed deeply. "Yeah."

'We're ready. Bring them up.'

• • • •

A few minutes later, the door knocked gently. Jane stayed seated and looked at me.

"You best answer it," she said.

My nerves returned, and I finished half a glass of prosecco in one go. Then stood up and went over to the door.

"Open it wide, be proud," she shouted from the living room.

I adjusted my robe, put my hand on the door handle and opened it wide as Jane had instructed. There stood my boyfriend and Rich, with their friends standing behind them. All of them looked stunned as I opened the door, and they caught a glimpse of me.

"Come in," I said warmly, turning and walking away, knowing they were watching me as they streamed silently through the door. I returned to sit with Jane, careful not to flash too much yet as I crossed my stocking-clad legs and my boyfriend, Rich, Ian, Dan, Joe, and Carl all went to stand in front of us. I was hoping Jane would speak. And she did.

"Hello, boys," she said, smiling at them all. "Get yourselves a drink and put the snacks out, and we can get started," she added.

They all turned and took the bags they were carrying to the bar area, putting lots of lager in the fridge with our prosecco and quickly arranging snacks all over the worktop. When they returned, Jane took control.

"So, everyone clear on what's going to happen?" she asked.

They all nodded.

"Don't forget. You wait for a nod. You'll get one, but you need to wait for it. We might be busy or overwhelmed. Okay?"

They nodded again.

"Okay then," she said, nodding to Rich and my boyfriend. They came over and stood before us, and we stood as planned. Rich in front of Jane and my boyfriend in front of me, we both stepped forward, and they took hold of us, kissing us and running their hands over our gowns. My boyfriend stopped kissing me briefly and whispered in my ear.

"Ready?"

"As I'll ever be, take off my gown," I replied quietly.

He reached down and undid the belt and slid it off my shoulders, leaving me standing in my basque, stockings and heels. He looked down.

"Fuck," he whispered. "You look utterly amazing."

"Thanks," I whispered sweetly. "Any preference on who you want to fuck me first?"

"Joe," he replied. "He thinks you're the most beautiful woman he's ever seen. He's right."

I smiled up at him. "Happy birthday," I whispered, then looked over his shoulder at his friend Joe, who was standing, clearly admiring my body, what he could see from behind my boyfriend. I nodded at him, and he walked through the crowd to where we stood. I don't have a clue where my character came from, but I adopted one, a sexy, sultry one.

"Hello, Joe," I said as he stood with us.

"Hi," he said a little nervously.

"He wants you to fuck me first. Would you like that?"

He nodded.

"Take a seat," I said to my boyfriend. He sat on the sofa where I had been just moments earlier as I turned to face Joe, who was looking more intently at my figure.

"Do you like my body?" I whispered.

"Yes," he said.

'You can have it just as soon as you're out of those clothes."

He looked at me, then at my boyfriend, who nodded. He removed his shirt, kicked off his shoes, and quickly removed his jeans and boxers. As he undressed, I looked to see what Jane was up to. She, too, had lost her robe and was approached by Alex as Rich sat down with my boyfriend.

Joe stood in front of me, naked, and his cock semi-hard. I stepped toward his body and looked up at him as I took his cock in my hand and slid my fingers down his length. It twitched and started to grow. I stepped back, crossed my legs, bent at my waist, lifted his cock and kissed it gently as my boyfriend watched, then stood back up and looked at my boyfriend, his eyes glistening.

"Your friend Joe is going to take me into the bedroom and fuck me," I whispered. "Wanna watch?"

"Maybe later," he said.

I smiled at him, knowing this was one of the things he wanted tonight. To sit and hear me being fucked from another room.

"Looks like it's just you and me then," I told Joe. "For now."

"See you later, honey," I said, taking Joe by the hand and leading him slowly to the bedroom as the audience watched. I showed him to one side of the enormous bed and sat on it. "Now, where were we?" I said, taking his cock once more and encouraging him forward. He didn't speak. He just took the hint and bought himself close to my mouth.

"I'll just get this hard, then my body is all yours, okay?" I said, looking up at him, his eyes sparkling with excitement. He nodded again. I kept eye contact with him as I lifted his manhood and slid it

44

into my mouth. He moaned a little as his cock became harder with every suck. When I was satisfied he was fully ready, I looked up at him as I lay back on the bed.

"As promised, Joe."

He leaned forward and cupped my breasts through my basque, then slid his hands down my body, parting my legs as he lifted them, exposing my pussy to him, and caressed them through my fishnet stockings. He knelt and eagerly buried his tongue inside me, making me moan. I looked around and caught glimpses of others standing around the edge of the room. They'd taken their clothes off and stood, some holding beer and almost all playing with their cocks as they watched. Then I felt the bed move as Jane sat on the other side. I couldn't see who was with her, but she was enjoying whatever they were doing to her.

Joe worked my pussy for a while. I wasn't getting any wetter. I couldn't, I'd arrived in the room as turned on as I had ever been, but I loved his tongue on my clit, and him stroking my legs eagerly as he worked. Eventually, he stood up, and I slid onto the bed properly, putting my head on the pillow. I lifted my knees and opened my legs, knowing everyone in the room would get their first glimpse of my pussy. I couldn't make their face out fully at this distance. It was a big room and was dim aside from the bedside lamps, but I heard approving murmurs as I opened my legs for them. Joe climbed onto the bed and slid between my legs, keen to take advantage of my willingness to let him fuck me. He leaned over me and waited briefly.

"No need to wait," I whispered eagerly.

He took hold of his cock and guided it into me. I whined in pleasure as he filled me with it and started to thrust. I closed my eyes briefly and moaned loudly as he penetrated me, becoming faster with each thrust. I had a realisation that I might come a lot tonight. As Joe pounded away at me, I felt something brush my hand, hanging off the edge of the bed. I looked over, and Dan was standing there. I took his cock in my hand and played with it as Joe continued to fuck me. It wasn't easy. Joe was forceful, in a good way. I was tiny, and his body moved mine as he impacted against me, driving himself into me and making it difficult to focus on what my hand was doing with Dan's cock.

Eventually, Joe slowed, eager to save himself, either for Jane or another turn with me. He kissed me on the cheek and withdrew. I sat up and eagerly took Dan in my mouth. He was already hard, and I wanted a cock inside me again, but I was happy to warm him up a little more. I looked up at him. "How do you want me?" I asked.

"On all fours," he replied.

"Oh, nice, yes, please," I replied, turning round and putting my knees on the edge of the bed and getting up so he could fuck me standing. I was just about to put my head down on the bed and accept him when I saw Ian looking at me. I couldn't help myself. I nodded, and he climbed onto the bed next to Jane, who was being fucked rather aggressively by Carl and screaming her head off and offered his cock to me. As I slid him into my mouth, Dan drove into me from behind, pushing my mouth onto Ian's cock and hitting the back of my throat. I gagged a little but didn't mind. Dan liked the sound of me gagging on his friend's cock, and grabbed my hips, slamming into me to drive Ian further into my mouth. After a few moments, I seemed to develop a skill for it, and both seemed very happy with the situation. I wasn't sure if Ian had been with Jane yet, but my gagging on his member made him tense, and he made no effort to withdraw. Instead, he put a hand on the back of my head, indicating his intent. I didn't care. No, I lied. I did care. I cared so much that I wanted him to come in my mouth while Dan fucked me. He started to groan, as did Dan. It was all too much for both of them and me, for that matter. My legs began to shake, an orgasm washing over me as they both came inside my body simultaneously. I couldn't concentrate on sucking Ian and let him drive his cock into the back of my mouth as he unloaded inside it, groaning wildly.

I couldn't scream from my orgasm. I wanted to, but my mouth was full of cock and come. Dan groaned loudly as he filled me with his load. He held my shaking body carefully, clearly realising I wasn't in complete control and could fall off the bed. Eventually, he withdrew, as did Ian. I swallowed Ian's come quickly, gasping for breath a little. I put my head down for a moment, still on all fours with my ass raised off the edge of the bed.

"Mind if I?" a voice asked.

I looked up. It was Rich. I liked fucking Rich, and I liked fucking. And I was here to fuck. No brainer.

"Not at all," I replied happily.

"Want me to give your pussy a break?" he asked softly. I knew instantly what he was asking.

"Okay," I replied eagerly.

As Rich went behind me and applied some lube to my rear, I looked at Jane being spit roasted by my boyfriend and Joe. She looked deliriously happy, and seeing her doing what I'd just done turned me on. Dan and Ian returned to the lounge, having finished in me, and Rich looked like he was almost done too. Leaving our boyfriends, Joe and Carl.

I felt Rich's cock pressing against my rear opening and closed my eyes as he slowly entered. I moaned loudly. Very loudly.

As Rich started to get up to speed in my rear, I noticed Carl go and stand behind him, watching Rich's cock disappearing into my tiny ass, clearly turned on by it as much as Rich and I were. He said something to Rich, but I didn't hear it. I was panting and moaning. Then I felt Rich withdraw, and Dan manhandled me onto my back quickly, lifted my legs, and slid himself into my pussy.

"Oh, hello, Dan," I panted as he started slamming into me with the same force I'd seen him fucking Jane earlier. It didn't take long before my legs shook, and I came again under the relentless fucking I was getting from Dan. He slowed a little, still not finishing, and I glanced at Jane. Clearly, the double penetration we had both tried last time we were together appealed to her, as she had just slid her body down onto Joe's cock as he lay on the bed, and I could make out my boyfriend putting some lube on her ass. Rich, Dan and I watched as my boyfriend slid into her.

"Oh, fucking hell," she shouted as he slid slowly into her ass. He stopped for a moment, giving her time to adjust, then she tapped his leg, and he and Joe started to fuck the hole they had each. Jane wailed in pleasure and threw her head back.

"Fancy it?" Rich asked from beside Dan, who was still inside me.

I did. I smiled.

Dan climbed onto the bed next to Joe, and I positioned myself in his lap next to Jane and easily slid him back inside my wet, come-drenched pussy lips. Rich was behind me quickly, and having already taken him in my back passage, I didn't need the warmup. He pressed against me, and there was little resistance as the tip of his cock disappeared inside my ass.

Jane held out a hand, and I took it as we enjoyed the four cocks fucking us.

Jane came first, screaming loudly, then me, also screaming. Then I felt Dan, who had been pushing his pelvis up from beneath me, started to tense. As he came, Rich put his hands on my shoulders and pressed my body down onto his cock as he thrust, pounding my ass in a way I'd never quite been able to manage before. Then he came, his come pouring into my rear. I glanced across. Joe and my boyfriend had finished inside Jane too.

Rich and my boyfriend removed themselves from our asses, and we lifted ourselves off Dan and Joe. The guys all got up, and Jane and I slumped on the bed as they left us to recover and headed to the lounge.

We both lay there next to each other, panting.

"I said this would be fucking amazing," Jane said.

"I'm a mess," I said, feeling myself dripping onto the bed.

"How many came in you?" Jane asked.

"One in my mouth, your boyfriend in my arse, and two in my pussy."

Jane smiled as if proud of me.

We should clean up. The guys are leaving shortly, and our men will want round two.

"So will I," I said, biting my bottom lip.

We undressed and had a quick shower together, then put on the hotel bathrobes and entered the lounge. All the guys were dressed and ready to leave. Jane and I worked our way around, hugging them all and saying thanks. Then they left.

Jane took off her bathrobe, naked underneath, and sat between our boyfriends. I took off mine and sat opposite them.

"I like having naked women wandering around the place," Rich said.

"Me too," my boyfriend added.

Jane beckoned me over, and I went and sat on her lap, both naked between our men.

"So, I'm planning on fucking this one shortly," Jane said to them, looking at me and running her hands through my hair. "Are you two coming too? Or are you sitting here drinking all night?"

My boyfriend looked across at us. "I think we should all fuck her brains out tonight. She doesn't seem to have had enough yet," he said.

"Neither have I," Jane said seductively. "We'll go and get started. Come when you're ready."

She stood me up and took my hand, leading me to the bedroom.

"But don't join us too soon," she shouted, closing the bedroom door behind her and pressing me against it.

"Now, let me get re-acquainted with this pussy," she said, sliding her fingers between my legs as I willingly opened them a little. "I've not been in here for nearly a month..."

I closed my eyes, and Jane went to work...

April 2008 – Cleansing

It ended.

Why?

Well, as much as I enjoyed the sex with my boyfriend and his friends. I didn't enjoy finding out he'd been screwing another girl. If he'd asked me, then maybe, especially if I was invited. But he didn't. Then he lied about it.

Game over.

Armed with what I'd learned during our time together (you'll remember the sexual adventures we had were enlightening for an inexperienced girl like me), I was preparing to head off to university myself—looking for more than just an education and a mountain of debt.

I'd become confident in my skin and immensely enjoyed showing a fair bit of it, at the right time, of course. My long legs, which I'd always considered spindly, were apparently beautiful, especially when most of their length was on show. As a result, short dresses and skirts passed for the daytime. Much shorter ones came out for evenings.

One night, before I left for university, I hit town one last time with a few friends. I wasn't looking for love...

At just over eighteen, feeling hot, looking hotter (at least I thought so), and armed with bucket loads of sexual frustration and a dress which left little to the imagination, I entered the one bar in town I knew I'd get to drink for free all night, and when I found a suitable candidate get some post-breakup-sex. What I wasn't planning on was getting quite a lot of it.

It was early in the night when he approached. He wasn't the first, but he was the first I'd consider. Looking back, I have a feeling it was bullshit, but at the time, a tale of being in the army, Twenty-three, and on leave did the trick. If I knew it, I'd tell you his name and his friends, but I never thought to ask.

51

He buys me drinks, asks me questions, and showers me with suggestive compliments. Standard stuff. He had me at "army", but I didn't let him know that.

Eventually, my friends drifted away with one-night stands of their own, spinning their tales in the hope of getting between my friend's legs at some stage.

Leaving me with him...

He'd been attentive, generous, and he was hot, so it was time to "give in" to his advances.

He started as they usually do—a hand on the small of my back, a few leg grazes, standard stuff. Then, eventually, he goes for pretty constant contact with me, advertising his "ownership" of this one to any other guys waiting to see if he was successful. I don't particularly like that these days, but I tolerated it at the time. It was standard practice amongst youngsters on a Saturday night.

We go outside, so he can smoke. It's quiet in the smoking area behind the bar. Quiet enough for me to open my body language a little and turn towards him more. It doesn't take him long to pull me forward and stick his tongue in my mouth. I reciprocate, and we kiss for quite a while. He feels my body. His hands feel strong, keen. My body responds to that, the temperature increasing inside my thong. I slide my hand up his shirt. It's chiselled under there. Maybe he is in the army? Perhaps I don't care.

"Wanna go somewhere quieter?" he asked.

"What do you have in mind?" I replied as he pressed his body against me and looked down into my eyes.

"I'm staying in town. My hotel is five minutes away."

I smile. "Lead the way."

As it turns out, it was five minutes for a guy in shoes. But when he's got a slightly drunk eighteen-year-old in high heels with him, it's more like fifteen. Especially when she encourages him to occasionally stop and grope her in shop doorways.

He was staying in one of those budget chain hotels that litter every town and city in the country. Each is the same. Clean, safe, and consistent.

Despite the alcohol and the desire for sex, I had enough about me to be considering my safety. And in that place, I felt I'd be safe.

We went through the lobby and up to his room, stopping in the stairwell for another fumble.

Through the door, click—time for sex.

I turned on him the moment the door was closed, unbuttoning his shirt as we stood outside the bathroom door, not even making it to the bedroom. He'd done this before, clearly, as he kicked off his shoes while I was removing his shirt. Good boy.

I pressed his shirt back over his shoulders and left him to do the rest while I moved on to his belt and jeans. He had them off in a flash. Stood in only his underwear, he lifted me, and I wrapped my legs around him as he kissed me and carried me over towards one of the double beds. He put me down, and I stepped back, peeling my tiny skin-tight dress over my head and casting it aside. I let him look at my slender body for a second, wearing only a thong and my heels, then sat on the edge of the bed.

He stepped between my open legs, clearly waiting to feel the warmness of my mouth around his cock. I didn't make him wait, yanking down his underwear and slipping his tip into my mouth. I held it there for a second, massaging it with my tongue, then parted my lips and slid my mouth down onto him.

"Holy shit." was all I heard as I closed my eyes and went to work.

At that point, a thought occurred to me. Only twelve months or so ago, I was a virgin. Things had changed a lot. Since then, I'd had a hell of a lot of sex with my ex before he went to university, then when I visited him, I'd had sex with him, a group of his friends, and one of his friend's girlfriends. And yet, right then, as I sat in nothing but a thong on a hotel bed with a stranger's cock deep in my mouth, I realised that this was only my second time one-to-one with a guy. The problem with that was I'd had wilder experiences which I loved and wanted to do more of, but on a one-night stand with someone you have just met, it's difficult to explain that you're into a "fair few things", and a quick fuck with a stranger is merely one of the more "vanilla" ones.

In any case, his cock was like a rod of iron in my mouth. And it was big. I enjoyed sucking on it so much I didn't want to stop, but he'd been looking at my body all night and wanted it.

Who was I to refuse?

He held my head and fucked my mouth a little, then lifted me off him. He cupped my small breasts with his strong hands, tweaked my nipples pleasantly, then knelt in front of me and pulled down my thong, revealing my completely shaven pussy. He looked up and smiled, then flicked the tip of his tongue over my clit. I bent a knee and whimpered.

He stood and lifted me in one impressive move and threw me onto his bed. I laughed as I landed, then looked up at the naked stranger, his well-built body ready to enter mine. I smiled at him and bit my bottom lip.

Guys like that.

Then I lifted my knees and parted my legs, giving him a full view of what was on offer.

He climbed up the bed slowly and buried his face into my pussy lips. I instinctively wrapped my legs around his head, pulling him in. He didn't disappoint, burying his tongue deep into me as I began to moan. He made me so wet, and my body ached to fuck.

I released my legs from around his head, and he wasted no time getting up and kneeling between them. In hindsight, I suspect he was waiting to be told to put on a condom. And, in hindsight, I should probably have told him to. But hindsight is a beautiful thing; instead, what I did next prevented him from having the choice.

I looked up at him, lifted my legs to either side of my chest, and held them there. I smiled once more. "What are you waiting for?"

I finished the sentence, just. Then I gasped as I felt his cock stretch my pussy as it entered. And I mean stretch. My eyes watered, but it was magnificent. And then, for the next however long (and I genuinely can't remember) — I loudly encouraged him to use my pussy, and he did. He fucked me in a way I'd never experienced before. He slammed into me with all his body weight repeatedly. I was yelping and screaming between moans. It was amazing. I can't remember how often he withdrew and moved my body into a different position so he could enter me again. The missionary was good, the doggy was great, lying on my side and hip holding my hip as he drove into me from behind was, well, you know.

I counted three orgasms before he even showed any signs of finishing. This was the workout I'd come out looking for that evening. But then he frustrated me. It didn't ruin everything, but I'd let him fuck me without a condom for a reason. I wanted him to fill me, load my tight pussy with his come. But he didn't.

He started to groan loudly. I moaned excitedly as I waited for his hot sticky gift to pump into me, and then he pulled out and came on my tummy.

Bastard.

Two things. Firstly, he didn't ask if I minded him making a mess of my body. Secondly, if he didn't want to fill my pussy, he could at least have had the decency to fill my mouth.

Yes, it was the right thing to do. But, meh.

I didn't make a big deal, naked, but for a pair of high heels in a stranger's hotel room. So, I got up and went to the bathroom to clean off his mess, at least satisfied that I'd had my brains well and truly fucked out on the way.

I wandered, tipsy and wobbly on my heels from all the leg shaking, back from the bathroom to find he had fallen asleep (really? a hot, horny, naked eighteen-year-old in your room?). I didn't need to go anywhere. I'd rigged my overnight absence with my parents. And I was tired, exhausted. So, I sat on the edge of the bed and took off my heels, then lay on top of the covers in the warm room for a while as he snored a little beside me.

I awoke at about 3 am to the sound of a click. I opened my eyes to see a guy standing by the other bed, lit only by the bathroom light streaming through the crack of the slightly open door, staring at me.

"Oh, sorry," he whispered. "We got split up, and he didn't tell me he wasn't alone."

My guy didn't stir, just carried on snoring quietly.

Given my sleepy state, it took me a second to realise I was facing this guy, lying on my side naked. That's a hell of an introduction.

He was older than me too. Mid-twenties, also good-looking. I shifted my leg slightly to cover my pelvis, and my hair mostly covered my chest. At that point, he couldn't see much more of me than if I was in the dress I'd gone out in. I smiled.

"It's okay. It happened quite quickly," I whispered.

He went into the bathroom. I was impressed. He is out drinking till 3 am, then returns from the club and remembers to brush his teeth before bed. He returned to the room in his boxer shorts and climbed into the spare bed, facing me.

"Did you have a good night?" I whispered.

"Yes, met up with some old friends. He was coming too, but a hot young brunette caught his eye."

"And then he ended up with me instead." I giggled.

"Did you have a good night?" he asked quietly.

I hesitated but didn't mean to. "Yes."

"But?"

"He fell asleep."

"Afterward, I hope?" he laughed, "No man could fall asleep during. Not with someone as attractive as you, I imagine."

I was flattered and a little turned on.

"After the first time, yes."

"Were you hoping for a second time then?"

I smiled and blinked. "Looks like that's not going to happen now, right?

"Because I came back?"

"Because he's fast asleep."

He paused. "Aren't you cold over there?"

"I am now, it was hot in here earlier, but I can't get in the bed because he's lying on most of the sheets."

He paused again, then looked up at me.

"There's room over here," he whispered.

I smiled across at him. "Are you trying to get me into bed?"

"Yes."

I brushed my hair back over my shoulder, exposing my chest a little and bit my lip again.

"Aren't you tired?" I asked.

"I'll stay awake all night if you want me to."

I slipped my legs off the bed into the gap between mine and his, then stood, the bathroom light illuminating my naked body as I took the two steps I needed to make it to the edge of his. He lifted the sheet, and I slipped in next to him, lying on my back as he lay beside me.

"Better?" he asked.

"Much," I replied. "How will I ever thank you?"

"I have a few ideas."

"Oh? like what?" I asked.

He reached over me, put his hand on my chin, and gently turned my head to face him. I smiled, waiting. He leaned down and kissed me.

He was gentler, softer than his friend, and it felt white hot at 3 am in that bed next to his sleeping friend.

He took his time. He knew he was in no rush. He slid his hands all over my chest, kissing my nipples and making them stand for him, then while he continued showing my upper body attention with his mouth, his hand strayed to my clit. I moaned softly as he explored me, parting my legs slightly to give him access to anything he wanted. His technique on my clit, which added to the atmosphere around us, was mind-blowing. he was intentionally being agonisingly slow. I loved and hated it at the same time.

I reached my hand inside his boxers and gently stroked his cock with my fingertips. If he was in no rush, neither was I. I slid my palm down his length and slowly played with his balls. I withdrew my hand and pulled suggestively at his waistband. He got the point, removing his hand from my clit, and disposing of his underwear.

I sat up, then leaned forward, lifting his cock into the air and circling it slowly with my tongue while he watched in the faint light.

"Fuck, I'd let you do that all night," he whispered. I looked into his eyes as I carried on, flicking my tongue over him, then smiled as I slowly slid him into my mouth.

"Let me return the favour," he whispered.

I shuffled around, keeping his cock in my mouth, as I lifted my leg over him and slowly lowered my pussy towards his mouth. He reached his arms around me and up towards my opening, then circled my wet pussy lips before sliding a few fingers inside me. I moaned and buried my mouth down deep onto his cock.

He withdrew his fingers and pulled at my back, encouraging me to lower myself onto him. As my pussy made contact with his mouth, I almost orgasmed immediately.

We sixty-nined for a while, a long while, slowly, neither of us in any rush. He gave me the slowest building orgasm of my life so far. When I eventually got there, I couldn't concentrate on his cock anymore. As I was approaching my orgasm, I was getting louder, and we had someone sleeping in the next bed. I didn't want to wake him. It might ruin my fun. So, I slipped one of his balls into my mouth and tried to be as quiet as I could as he pushed me over the edge. I ground my pelvis into his mouth hard, and he responded by maintaining my orgasm, clearly enjoying having my body shuddering uncontrollably on top of his.

When I released the pressure of my pussy on his face, he slowed, giving me time to recover. I lifted my head and wiggled my lower body over him.

"Wow," he whispered.

I spun around, sat on him just above his waist, and looked at him. His eyes were glistening.

I slowly slid myself backwards until my pussy was on top of his cock. I ground down a little.

"Mind if I drive?" I whispered.

"Not at all," he replied.

I cast a look at his sleeping friend. I didn't ride his cock earlier. I didn't get the chance.

I lifted my pelvis slightly and slipped my hand between my legs, raising his cock into position at my opening, and then I slowly sat back down.

He sighed. "You feel amazing."

I pressed down, taking his entire length. The pressure of his cock against my cervix made me breathe deeply. "You don't feel too bad yourself," I replied, moving my pelvis in circles. He reached up his hands to give me some support. I took them and leaned onto them so I could rise and fall onto his rock-solid cock with ease.

We stared into each other's eyes. This was a record. I'd met him half an hour ago, and here I was with his cock deep inside me. I didn't care. He was giving me what I needed, and despite being less physically aggressive than my fucking at the hands of his friend a few hours ago, it was better. Much better.

As I rode his cock, we both became a little louder. Too loud. His sleeping friend rolled over and slowly opened his eyes.

I have to wonder what he thought at that moment. The hot young thing he'd spent the evening trying to get into bed, then had sex with only a few hours ago, was in front of him, panting as she rode his friend's cock on a bed two feet away. He had no emotional attachment to me, nor me to him. But it could have gone very badly. Thankfully, it didn't.

He opened his eyes wider and watched as his teenage conquest slid eagerly up and down on his friend's cock. I looked across at him and smiled. His hand went to his cock, and he started playing with himself as my attention returned to the guy whose cock was satisfying me immensely with every grind of my pelvis.

I loved the thought of him watching, enjoying, and playing with himself. I loved the sex I was getting. There was just one more thing I needed. I reached behind and down my back, cupping his balls as I bounced on his cock.

"Empty these into me," I panted, allowing myself to speak (and moan) louder since everyone in the room was now awake.

"I thought you would never ask," he said, lifting my body off his by my hips and rolling me onto my front, my face looking squarely into the eyes of the man I'd had sex with just a few short hours ago. He pulled me up onto my knees by my hips, then held them as he slid his cock into me once more.

I don't know if it was pity, guilt, or greed, but I felt a little sorry for his friend, lying on the bed two feet away, jerking off while his friend was preparing to come in my pussy. I looked into his eyes and opened my mouth. He got the point, rising to his feet and standing between the beds. I raised onto my elbows, and he slid his cock into my mouth, holding my head as he slid into it repeatedly.

I came first. Being spit-roasted by two exceptionally fit and good-looking guys was precisely what I needed to form new erotic memories and banish some of the ones of my ex. My legs started to shake, and it was all I could manage not to bite the cock in my mouth. My cock-muffled screams brought the guys to where they needed to be quickly and, thankfully, almost simultaneously. The moment I felt the familiar change in rhythm (that all guys do as they prepare to come) from the newcomer in my pussy, I squeezed my pussy walls onto his cock as his fluid started to flow into me. He thrust repeatedly, forcing me onto his friend's cock and making me gag a little. He finished giving me his load and slowed but remained inside me, rocking slowly as he watched my head bobbing up and down on his friend.

"Can I"? his friend asked.

"Mmmm," I replied, going deep on him.

He held my head tightly and grunted, filling my mouth with relentless streams. So much so that I had to swallow mid-way to accept it all. But I managed it.

They both withdrew from my body, and I flopped onto the bed, panting but finally satisfied. I realised they were looking down at me, wondering what to do.

"There's two of you, two beds, and only one of me," I said, still breathing deeply. "If we're doing this again before I go home in the morning, then you two can fight over which bed I'm sleeping between you in while I have a quick shower and clean up. Okay?"

They nodded, clearly excited at the thought of enjoying me again.

I stood up in front of the first guy I'd had sex with that evening and looked up into his eyes.

"And next time, don't ask. Just come in me, not on me. I don't mind where."

March 2008 and October 2010 – His father

After my ex and I had split up, I was finishing my last year of school before University, and he was miles away, fucking his new blonde at his University. I had some of his stuff, you know, like you do, in my bedroom. I wanted it gone. I had to agree it with him, so we texted a little, arranging for me to take it to his house while his Dad was there one Saturday afternoon. His parents were in the middle of a divorce themselves. His mum had been seeing someone behind his father's back (like mother, like son!), so his father was living alone in the family home.

I'd always liked his father, Paul. To look at, he was an older version of my ex in almost every way. Of course, this made him attractive to me, as I was attracted to his son. We got on well for the year I'd been seeing his son, and he seemed really nice. So, on Saturday, as agreed, I picked up my "ex-box" (see what I did there?") and took it round to his house.

His father, Paul, opened the door and took the box.

"Hi Pixie, fancy a drink while you're here?" Paul asked, happy to see me. I don't know how or why, but at some stage, while I was dating his son, he'd decided to call me Pixie. He was the only one that did, and I quite liked it.

"He's definitely not here, is he?" I asked, not really trusting my ex any more.

"No, just me."

I smiled, stepped into the house, and followed him to the kitchen. He put the kettle on while I leaned against the countertop, staring out the kitchen window.

"I'm sorry about what happened," he said, distracting me.

"Don't be. It wasn't your fault," I said, shrugging it off. "Besides, I'm fine. Really. How are you doing, you know, with the divorce?"

"Looks like I get to keep the house," he replied. "We're just sorting everything else now. It takes ages," he said, sighing, looking sad.

I felt a bit sorry for him. Granted, we had both been cheated on, but I was eighteen. I was already eyeing all the opportunities a sexy little brunette had before her. His wife had left him for another man, a younger man, and he was starting over again in many ways. I put down my mug and went over to give him a hug. That's all. A hug. He put his mug down too, and as I put my arms around his waist, turned my head, and pressed it against his chest, he nervously put his hands on my shoulders.

Guess how I felt? – Yeah – you got it. He smelled great, looked good, and knew how to hug. The hug lasted longer than it should have, and I felt a familiar welcome stirring in my body. Eventually, he forced himself to let go. At least, that's how I see it. He may have been pushing me to let go – I can't remember. We returned to our coffees, but it was too late for me. He had turned my head and awakened something inside me. I looked up at him, trying to seduce him with my eyes. I'd never given sex with an older man a thought before, but at that moment, it was all I could think about. I guess my gentle flirting was starting to work. If it weren't for that fucking phone call, I'd have easily convinced him to take me to bed.

Instead – annoyingly – his wife rang about the divorce. Nothing pours cold water on a guy thinking about fucking his son's eighteen-year-old hot ex-girlfriend like arguing over a divorce. As soon as I recognised her voice and saw his body language change, I knew it was time to leave. I smiled at him sweetly, then made my exit. Frustrated isn't the word. I'm pretty sure that was the first time I'd wanted sex and not had it. I had to satisfy myself when I went home, slipping into the bath with my rabbit and making myself come thinking about him. I did that a lot over the following months and years, despite everything (and everyone) else I got up to. He was the one that got away, the mystery, the one I thought about when I was alone in my bed naked, the one perhaps I'd never see again.

Two years later, at University myself by that stage, I came home for the weekend for my Dad's fiftieth birthday party. It coincided with my twentieth. I didn't want a joint party but had agreed to a birthday cake with twenty candles at my Dad's party. I came home Friday lunchtime, and the garden was already set up. We weren't rich by any standards, but my family home was quite large, and we had a massive garden which was great for entertaining if the British weather would allow. This weekend, it did. Unseasonably for British summer, it was warm and dry, and the sun was out, so there were chairs and tables, a barbecue, and all the regular stuff set out. At about five, people started to arrive.

My mum dragged me from table to table, introducing me to new people and re-introducing me to people I hadn't seen in years. She gushed about how proud she was that I had gone to University and showed me off as mums do. I did the dutiful daughter thing, then joined my Dad at the barbecue for a break. As we stood there, watching a vast collection of meat cooking, a voice behind us nearly made my chest explode excitedly.

"Is that you, Pixie?"

I turned slowly, and Paul was standing before me, as handsome as the day I left his house two years ago.

"Pixie?" my Dad asked, laughing.

"He came up with it while I was dating his son," I said, smiling. My Dad looked at Paul.

"She was tiny. She'd turn up to our house in little dresses with bows in her hair and just float around the place. Seemed to fit." My Dad saw the funny side.

"She's still tiny," my Dad replied, returning to his barbecue.

Armed with two years more confidence and delighted to see him again, I wandered over to Paul, and we walked to an empty table.

"So, did the divorce go okay in the end?" I asked.

"Hardly. But it's done now," Paul replied. "I see you're still as beautiful as ever. Boyfriend?"

"Nah, not at the moment," I said sweetly. "Have you found anyone yet?"

"I've not really been looking yet," he replied casually.

"Did you keep the house?" I asked. Making a point of not asking about my ex.

"Oh, yes. Not much else, though," he laughed.

"The last time I saw you, we were standing in your kitchen having a cuppa, and then your ex-wife called."

"And ruined it," he whispered.

"Ruined what?" I asked, flirting a little and smiling at him.

"It was nice having you around," he said, avoiding answering. I liked that. It made me more curious.

My mother interrupted us again, and I spent another hour or so being dragged around meeting people, making occasional eye contact with Paul as I moved around groups of people. There was something there. I knew it. I just needed to find an opportunity to explore it. Eventually, later in the evening, I found my way back to Paul.

"I never did finish that cuppa you made me," I said softly.

"I washed it up, sorry Pixie, it was two years ago," he laughed.

I leaned in seductively and whispered. "Then maybe you could make me another sometime?"

Now, I knew that he knew that I was offering him sex. He couldn't miss the signs, and he didn't. His response was perfect.

"What are you doing tomorrow?" he asked.

"I'm out with a few friends tomorrow night but nothing during the day. I'm not going back to University till Sunday."

He looked around to make sure nobody was listening.

"Fancy a cuppa around midday?"

"Perfect," I replied. "I'll see you then."

I left him to mingle with his friends, smiling as we avoided each other for the rest of the evening.

The following day, I was up early, showered, shaved my legs – amongst other things, and ironed my outfit before my parents managed to drag themselves out of bed. Then at around eleven forty-five, I grabbed my little rucksack and headed out of the house – to the library, apparently, with some Uni work to do.

I walked the ten minutes to Paul's house, which looked exactly as I remembered it, and strolled up and knocked on the door nervously.

He answered the door wearing a pair of jeans and a white T-shirt. Classic, I thought. I stepped in quickly, he closed the door behind me, and we headed to the kitchen. He put the kettle on and then turned to look at me. I'd opted to walk to his house in tight black jeans and a fitted white blouse. This clearly wasn't what he'd hoped for, and I knew it.

As the kettle boiled, I decided to spring my surprise before we'd said more than hello.

"Mind if I use your bathroom while you make the drinks?" I asked sweetly as he looked at me nervously across the kitchen.

"Of course. I assume you remember where it is?" he asked.

"Yeah, think so,"

Of course, I knew. I'd walked across the landing naked to that bathroom often enough as an eighteen-year-old to wipe his son's come from my pussy. I'd given my first blow job, swallowed my first mouthful of semen, lost my virginity, and had my first anal sex in that house. But none of that with him.

I entered the bathroom, removed my jeans and blouse, and pulled a perfectly ironed, folded, ludicrously short white summer dress from my rucksack. I took off my underwear and slipped it on. Then I put my hair up in bunches, packed everything, shoes included, into my backpack, and left it in the bathroom for later. I strolled barefoot back down the stairs, wearing absolutely nothing but my dress and a smile.

I breezed into the kitchen and stood next to him. He turned and looked down at me. My long slim legs were exposed entirely, the buttons at the top of my dress mostly open and barely covering my breasts. He looked stunned.

"Return of the Pixie," I said sweetly, taking a mug.

"Pixie didn't dress in anything quite that short," he whispered. "Unfortunately."

"She does now," I said, walking away and leaning against the countertop exactly where I had almost two years ago. Paul admired me, I saw it, and I liked it. We faced each other, mostly drinking our tea in silence, smiling at each other as he studied my legs and seemed to undress me with his eyes.

Let's review before it gets messy – because you know it will. Paul was the divorced father of my ex. He looked like my ex, in a good way, but was more handsome, more rugged, and at the time around thirty years older than me, which made him at least 25 years older than the oldest guy I'd slept with up until that point. I was just twenty years old and reasonably sexually experienced. I had come here to let this sexy older many do with me as he pleased. There was something sexy about wanting him, but there was also something sexy about fucking my ex's Dad, regardless of how much I genuinely liked him. Put the two together, and it was a pretty explosive situation. Though I didn't expect what was to come (if you pardon the pun). Time for Pixie to get her lot...

I put my mug on the worktop next to me and bent a knee slightly as he continued looking at me. I stared into his eyes and put my hands on the worktop on either side of me.

"Expecting visitors today?" I asked sweetly.

"No," he said, eyes glistening.

"So we have all afternoon?"

"Yes."

I lifted the bent knee further, placing my foot on my other knee, my leg closer to him.

"So, Paul. Are you going to take this dress off, or am I?" I said softly.

He looked at me and smiled, finding a confidence I'd never seen from him.

"You take it off, Pixie," he said.

At that moment, I decided that the dominant older man turned me on.

I continued learning against his kitchen countertop and slowly raised my hands to the buttons on my dress. One by one, I undid them. The first few gave him his first sight of my breasts. His eyes studied them eagerly. Then the next few revealed my stomach, which he also studied and waited for more. Then the last three revealed my freshly shaven pussy. When I had finished the last button, I stood away from the countertop and let the dress fall to the kitchen floor, leaving me completely naked in front of him.

"Come here," he said firmly.

I walked towards him, stopping within reach. He reached up and cupped my chin, lifting my head to look into his eyes, slid his hand down and circled a nipple with his fingertips, then gave it a firm squeeze. I sighed, a little in shock, a little in pain, and a lot in pleasure. He ran his hand down my body slowly and brushed against my clit. I sighed again as I stood there, hands behind my back, offering my naked body to him. He walked around behind me, studying me. He slid his hand down my back and between my ass cheeks. I leaned forward a little instinctively as he studied my ass.

"What's on offer?" he asked, squeezing my ass cheek and moving back around in front of me.

"Everything you see," I said softly.

"Everything?"

"Everything."

He smiled. "It's a good thing we have all afternoon."

This wasn't the Paul I knew, the Paul I thought I'd come here to have sex with. This was Paul 2.0, the upgraded version. He had fire and desire in his eyes. I had a feeling that when he'd finished with my body, the walk home from his house might take longer than the walk here. I hoped so, at least.

"Come on," he said, taking my hand and leading me from the kitchen. We went upstairs and into his bedroom, where there was a large modern, four-poster bed. I scanned the room. On his bedside table stood a box of condoms and some lube – I liked that he had prepared, and there was a door leading to an ensuite – giving me an exit to clean up any cum-filled orifices he kindly created this afternoon. I was becoming too horny for words.

He let go of my hand, and I stood near the bed. I thought it best not to get on it yet, and await further instructions. He took off his T-Shirt and stepped in behind me again, running his hands over my small breasts and tweaking my nipples roughly. This was new for me and very welcome indeed. I tilted my head back and looked up at him. He leaned down, kissed me, and continued roughly playing with my nipples, making me moan through the kiss.

My usual instinct of dropping to my knees and taking cock in my mouth didn't seem to be an option, at least not yet. Paul was initially interested in exploring my body. Possibly because he'd fixated on it so many times in the past. I wasn't about to stop him. Over the next fifteen minutes, I learned something about older men. Or, possibly about younger men. This wasn't a rush to breed me or quick foreplay to convince me to open my legs. Paul wanted to explore me. Every last inch of me. And I loved every second of it. As we kissed endlessly, he simply stroked my torso, my breasts and occasionally my clit. Eventually, he turned me to face him, then continued kissing me deeply as he put his hands on my ass cheeks and lifted me. I instinctively wrapped my legs around my waist and arms around his neck. I thought he would carry me somewhere, but he didn't. Instead, he just stood there, with little me wrapped around him. The way he held me put his fingertips near my pussy lips, teasingly close. But he didn't move them. He just gripped my ass and kept me in place. Moments later, he turned and carried me to the bed. He lowered me down gently, and I sat on the edge of it. I thought this was the perfect moment for him to feel my lips around his cock, but he still didn't offer it. He pressed my shoulders back gently, and I lay down. He lifted my legs and started to kiss one all over, from my ankle up, until I could feel his body head near my clit, and then he started again with the other. It was equally erotic and frustrating at the same time. When he'd finished with my legs, he nodded to the pillows. I scooted back onto his bed and lat in the middle of it, my legs straight and closed initially. He climbed onto the bed and lay on me, kissing my neck, then my collarbone. He licked and sucked on my nipples, then bit each gently, sending electricity through my body. Then he kissed my tummy. Then he looked up, that fire still burning in his eyes.

"I want to taste you, Pixie," he said.

I smiled down at him and threaded my legs between his arms, opening them and giving him unrestricted access. He looked down, studying my sex.

"That looks so perfect, Pix. I may be a while."

"Take as long as you need," I whimpered, lying my head back on the pillow and waiting.

He wasn't lying. As I lay there, I could feel the warmth of his breath inside my legs as he studied his long-awaited prize. Then I felt a soft kiss on my clit, and finally, his tongue slid between his lips and then between mine. We both moaned a little. He slid his tongue upward and started to massage my clit very slowly. I ran my hands through his hair, panting softly as he steadily increased the pressure of his tongue on my clit. He slid a hand up my leg and pressed it upward a little as he slowly slid back down to my opening and slipped his tongue into me.

"Holy fuck," I whispered. I heard Paul snigger a little, then press my other leg upward. I lifted them and held my knees on either side of my chest for him to have full access.

"You did say everything is on offer, didn't you?" he said, kissing my pussy lips.

"God, yes," I replied.

He kissed downward and drew a circle around my rear with his tongue, then placed a hand on each ass cheek and spread them as he buried it in my ass.

"Oh, god," I whimpered, aching my pelvis upward to encourage him. He let go of my ass cheeks and looked up at me, smiling as he slid two fingers into my pussy, then withdrew them and pressed them against my ass. My body offered little resistance as his fingers slid inside. I was just getting to grips with the fantastic sensation of him fingering my ass when he buried his tongue in my clit again, making me shudder with pleasure and cry out happily. He continued for a few moments, then slowed and removed his fingers, looking up at me as he kissed my clit a little.

"I've wanted you every day since you came round here two years ago," he said, smiling.

"Me too," I replied.

I sat up slowly as he removed his tongue from me and knelt before me. I slid my hand over the bulge in his jeans. He was clearly already hard for me.

"It's getting tight for space in there," I said sweetly, reaching for his belt. "How about we let him out to play?"

I opened his belt and jeans quickly, kissing his cock through his boxer shorts. He stood up and took the rest of his clothes off quite quickly, then knelt back in front of me, his large rigid cock right before my face, a little pre-come glistening at the tip. I licked it off and swallowed it quickly.

"I hope there's more where that came from?" I asked, lifting my hand and cupping his balls.

"Plenty for you, Pixie," Paul replied, eyes glistening.

I smiled as I pulled my legs beneath me and sat comfortably in front of him, keen to give him a long slow blow job to return the attention he'd lavished on my body so far. I removed my hand from his balls and kissed them softly, then sucked them into my mouth one at a time. It was his turn to start cursing.

"Fucking hell, Pix," he said breathlessly, putting his hands on his hips.

Then I put the tip of my tongue between them and drew a line to the tip of his cock. I looked into his eyes, opened my mouth, and slowly took him inside. I tried desperately to remain slow, but by now, I was so horny that my inner porn star was fighting to get out. I held his cock shallow in my mouth and flicked my tongue over him, then slowly bobbed my head up and down, taking as much of it as I could sitting as I was. It was no use, though. I was too horny. Porn star P won the battle.

"Want to have some real fun?" I asked cheekily.

"What do you have in mind?" he asked curiously.

"Jump off the bed a second," I said excitedly. Paul climbed off, and I lay back, my head off the edge of the bed. "Now fuck my mouth," I said sweetly.

He stepped forward and slid his cock into my mouth. "Okay?" he asked.

I muttered, "Mmmmm," and put my hands on his ass, pulling him deeper. He pressed, and I relaxed, letting him into my throat.

"Holy fucking Christ," he said as my lips reached his pubic bone. I pressed against his thighs gently, and he withdrew, letting me up for air. I coughed a little.

"Now you know how it works. When I want air, I'll push you back. Otherwise, go for it," I whispered, smiling.

He crouched down a little, held my head between his hands, and steadily drove his length back into my waiting and willing throat. Once deep, he started to fuck. He took advantage of my offer for a few minutes, fucking my face harder and hard throughout, but nothing I didn't like. Eventually, his breathing changed, and he pulled out.

"I'm gonna come if we do that much longer," he said, holding his cock and staring at me. I rolled over onto my front and lifted onto my elbows.

"And what's the problem with that?" I asked, licking my lips.

"Don't you want to?..."

"Fuck?" I said casually. "Yes, I do. But I hadn't anticipated this being a one-shot deal. You have me all day, and if I cancel my night out, you can have me all night too." I said, bending my legs and pointing my toes to the ceiling as his eyes sparkled. "That work for you?"

"Of course!" he said, laughing.

"Good, now bring that cock over here and come in my mouth."

You can imagine. I didn't need to tell him twice.

As I lay on the bed on my front, propped up on my elbows, he came at me with his cock again, and I wasted no time getting to work on it. I only wanted to taste him by this point, and he was already on the edge. I clamped my mouth around him and sucked his manhood for all I was worth, with a bit of help from his hand on the back of my head. It took a minute, maybe too, for his breathing to change again.

"I'm coming, Pixie," he whispered.

"Mmmm," I muttered.

He groaned and went shallow, waiting for my mouth to fill.

"Fuck," he shouted loudly as he started to shake a little, and my prize flowed into my mouth. Streams of his salty gift pulsed into my little mouth. When it stopped, I slowly lifted off him and looked up. I opened my mouth to show him what he'd given me, then closed it and swallowed it eagerly.

He looked down into my eyes, satisfied. "Why my boy let you go is beyond me," he said, stroking my hair. I smiled at him.

"If he hadn't, we wouldn't be here now."

I stood off the bed and gave him a hug. "Why don't I go and make coffee, then you can fuck me?"

He beamed. "You're amazing."

I wandered off naked as he climbed onto his bed. I turned at the door to see him watching me and wiggled my rear as I left to make drinks.

Fifteen minutes later, I'd returned with the coffee, and we were sat naked on his bed, drinking our coffees, when something needed to be discussed.

"I notice you have prepared," I said, picking up the unopened box of condoms I'd spied earlier on his bedside table. He smiled.

I turned to face him, lifting my leg a little and putting my hand on his soft cock and stroking it gently. "Well, it's entirely up to you, but don't think you need them on my account," I said, looking into his eyes sheepishly.

"I thought you might want them," he said curiously.

"I want to feel this inside me," I said, leaning down and kissing his cock. "Not one of these. But if it makes you feel more comfortable."

He took the box of condoms from me and threw it across the room to make a point. I smiled on the inside and the outside. His mobile rang, and he picked it up, looking at the screen.

"It's your ex," he said calmly.

"Answer it," I whispered seductively. "Tell him you have just fucked my throat and come in my mouth."

"Maybe not," he laughed, answering the phone.

I sat naked next to my ex's father while they chatted on the phone. It wasn't a short call. He'd called his Dad to catch up. Horny, and frustrated that my ex was stopping me from getting what I wanted, I decided to enjoy myself a little.

I lay beside Paul and put my leg across him, drawing circles on his chest with a fingertip. He looked at me and smiled, amused as he continued his conversation. I decided to up my game, and I got up, threw a leg over him, and sat down on his soft cock, then started gyrating my pelvis on him slowly, his cock lying beneath me, massaging my clit as I slid forwards and back. My clit was already sensitive from his tongue earlier, so it didn't take long for me to start whimpering softly as I used his cock to pleasure it. It also didn't take long for his cock to respond., partly from what I was doing and partly from Paul watching his little Pixie gyrating naked on him. I lifted my hands into my long brown hair and closed my eyes as I moaned softly. I felt his spare hand reach up and caress my breast, but they carried on talking. Time to take things further.

I slid forward on his now-hard cock and took it in my hand, positioned it at my opening, and looked down at him. His eyes sparkled, but he shook his head no. I nodded yes, and smiled. I slid my pelvis back, his cock entering and stretching me, taking my breath away.

"I need to go. Something's come up," Paul said to my ex quickly as I sat my weight onto him, taking his entire length, panting softly. "Yeah, speak soon." He hung up and threw his phone on the floor.

"Something's come up, has it?" I asked cheekily, shifting my hips and taking my breath away again.

"You feel amazing, Pix,"

"It seems I fit just like a glove," I said ecstatically, at the perfect amount of stretch his cock provided me. I put my hands on his chest and rocked a little, moaning softly. He sat up and, in one easy move, spun us and lay me back on the bed. I giggled.

"So you do want to fuck me then?" I asked sweetly.

"What do you think?" he asked, leaning down and kissing me, holding still. Mid-kiss, Paul withdrew to his tip and drove into me. I cried out with pleasure and gripped his sheets as I felt his weight land on my pelvis.

"Let me know if I get carried away. I've been fantasising about you for years," he whispered.

"Paul,"

"Yes?"

"Get carried away."

He did. I can honestly say that it was that sex, that afternoon with Paul, that genuinely changed my sex life. Yes, I'd had some pretty wild adventures to that point. Still, there was something about this particular sex that opened my eyes – and my legs – to rough, carnal sex.

He lifted my legs onto his shoulders and drove himself into me like a man possessed. He built me to orgasm like none I had before, and then he kept me there, shaking and screaming as he pounded my little body. The only respite from his onslaught of pleasure was when he would occasionally move position. Each position was intense, and no matter how we did it, he drove into me in a way that made my toes curl continually. Despite our height difference, he even managed to press me against the wall and fuck me standing up. I can't tell you (because I can't remember) how many orgasms I had over the next thirty minutes or so. My pussy was soaking by the time we returned to the bed, and he lay me back down and entered me again.

He was slower but just as deep, and I felt he had his reasons.

"Are you gonna come in me?" I asked softly as I moaned endlessly.

"Yes, and I want to look into your eyes as I fill you," he said.

"I looked up at him, moaning softly as he started to moan.

"I'm ready. Give it to me," I whispered.

He withdrew, groaned, and slid in. His cock pulsing his load deep inside my pussy as he looked into my eyes. I smiled, happy at the thought of his seed inside my body.

He held me for a moment, then withdrew his cock and lay beside me, both out of breath. I kissed him briefly, then skipped off to his ensuite, tidied myself up a little, then went back to bed, cuddling up to him. We lay together, kissing and cuddling, then drifted off to sleep.

I was first to wake, about an hour or so later. I looked at my phone; four-thirty in the afternoon. I only had a little while before I needed to go home and change to go out, but I also wanted to stay. I texted my friends that something had come up and agreed to meet them for lunch the following day before I went back to University. I put my phone down and turned to look at him. His eyes were open, and he was smiling.

"What time is it?" he asked.

"Half four," I replied, snuggling up to him.

"Shit. I suppose you have to go."

"About that," I said softly. "Did you have plans for tonight?"

"No, why?"

"I wondered if you might want to keep me a while longer?"

"But you have plans?"

"I had plans."

"So you can stay?"

"All night. If you want me to?"

"Oh, Pixie, you're a dream," he said, reaching over and stroking my shoulder.

"We're going to need to get up and eat, though. If you want to have sex with me all night, I will need some energy," I said, seductively laying out my intent for the evening.

He smiled. "Take away?"

"Works for me."

We lay there a little longer, relaxing in bed, and then I went for a shower to make myself all fresh for the evening while Paul put on his bathrobe and ordered Chinese. I slipped my little white "Pixie" dress back on while we ate, nothing else, which allowed me to give him the occasional flash of my pussy and ass, which seemed to have the desired effect. I also liked that he didn't dress and stayed in his robe, indicating our shared intentions.

After dinner, we sat on the sofa watching tv, and I lay next to him, my head in his lap. I was still horny, and feeling playful, so as he watched TV, I casually lifted my head, undid his robe, and lifted his soft cock into my mouth, sucking it slowly. It was as much for me as for him, I loved sucking cock, and I had no intent of this turning into anything more than my sexy older man enjoying his little Pixie sucking on him for a while. He traced his finger down my back and lifted my skirt, stroking my bare ass as he pretended to be watching TV. I opened my legs a little, just in case there was anything he wanted. He responded by slipping his hand between my ass cheeks and probing around my pussy lips a little, making me wriggle as I continued slowly enjoying his growing cock. He eventually slid his fingers upward, gently teasing my rear opening, which he had fingered many hours ago. I had a feeling he wanted it. At least, I hoped he did.

I looked up from his cock. "Did you want to complete your collection?" I said sweetly.

"What?" he asked, clearly checking we were on the same page.

"Well, you have come in my mouth, you have come in my pussy, it only seems right you should come in my ass too. Don't you think?" I said, smiling and returning to sucking his cock. He slid a finger into my wet pussy and removed it again, lubricating it just enough to slide into my ass. I didn't flinch. I just carried on licking his shaft as my body welcomed him in. I moaned a little.

He picked up the remote and turned off the TV. "I think we need to take this upstairs," he said.

I lifted my head off his cock.

"I thought you would never ask," I replied as he removed his finger from my rear, and I stood up. I took his hand and led him upstairs, unbuttoning my dress with my spare hand as we walked. I'd undone it by the time we were back in his bedroom. I let it fall to the floor as I walked over to his bedside table and picked up his bottle of lube. I went over to him and pushed the shoulders off his already open robe, and it fell, his cock hard and ready for action. I turned my back to him and leaned forward as we stood there, squeezed some lube into the palm of my hand and massaged it into my ass while he watched silently. Then I turned back to him and rubbed the rest into the entire length of his cock.

"We need to make sure you can get all the way in, right?" I said, looking down at the glistening cock about to take my ass. I stood on my tiptoes and kissed him, then turned and walked to his bed, climbing onto it on all fours, then put my head down on the duvet, my slim ass in the air, waiting for him.

I didn't look up. I just waited and felt the bed move as Paul climbed onto it. He stroked my ass cheeks gently, then pressed the tip of his cock against me. I pushed back against him a little, helping him to pass the first hurdle as my ass relaxed and his cock inched in. I yelped a little, then moaned as he patiently waited for me to adjust to the fleshy intruder in my ass. As he held still, I slowly inched backwards until I had all of him inside me.

"Now, over to you," I whispered through my panting.

Paul withdrew slightly and slowly rocked back and forth. It didn't take him long to realise I was capable and willing for more, and he moaned as he upped his pace.

"Fucking hell, your ass feels amazing, Pixie," he moaned.

He fucked me for a while, getting more and more animated quickly as the tightness of my ass and the intensity of the whole experience made us moan loudly. I knew, this time at least, he wouldn't last as long as he had earlier. I slid forwards, and he withdrew, then rolled over and pully my legs up.

"Come in my ass, Tony," I insisted as he took up his position at my rear again. He slid back in, pressing my legs up further and fucking me hard. As he'd taken my legs, I rubbed my clit as he pounded into me, making myself come in front of him, screaming in pleasure and squeezing his cock with my ass as I did. That was all Tony needed. He grunted loudly, slammed into my ass, and pumped his load into my back passage as he carried on thrusting, seemingly unwilling to stop. Eventually, he slowed, both of us out of breath, and withdrew, lying next to me as I gingerly lowered my legs onto the bed.

When we'd recovered a little, I slid over to him and put a leg across him once more as he stroked my shoulder.

"Pix, you're giving me memories I'm going to remember for a very long time," he said softly.

I left my head on his chest, not looking up.

"I could write a book. My night with Pixie," he sighed happily.

"Nights," I said softly.

"What?" Paul asked.

I lifted my head and looked into his eyes. "You live alone, we're both single, and I love you fucking me. I was thinking earlier that until one of us isn't single any more, maybe whenever I come home for the weekend, I could come around for a cuppa?"

"You want to do this again?" he asked, both excited and surprised.

"And again and again," I replied, smiling. "If you want to?"

"If I want to? Pixie, you have no idea how much I want to."

"Then it's settled. I'll dig out some more of my Pixie dresses, then each time I'm home, I'll come round, and you can fuck my brains out all night. Deal?"

"Deal," he replied.

That was all it took. We were completely relaxed in each other's company from then on. The fact that this was the house where I'd lost my virginity to his son and had sex countless times in the next bedroom as a teenager didn't matter. We never discussed it, or his son, again. Throughout the rest of that night, we had sex in the shower and in bed again. The following day I was woken by a hard cock pressing against my pussy lips – which, of course, I welcomed in immediately - and later, I treated myself to one last mouthful of his come in the kitchen before I left.

He was old enough to be my Dad and over thirty years older than me. But, you know what? I really didn't care. I left for University, already planning to return for another night with Paul a few weeks later. It became a regular thing.

November 2010 – Pixie, Nymph, and the older man.

I was never one to flaunt my sexual exploits. You'll notice, if you have been keeping up, that despite the highly erotic nature of my liaisons, only once did I do the classic 'girl meets guy, girl fucks guy' - and even then, it was hardly traditional. I screwed his friend too.

I carefully planned everything so that my public life and my sex life rarely met. My University friends saw me as a 'girl-next-door' type. But with a filthy sense of humour.

Imagine my surprise then when one Thursday night, while I was curled up on my bed in my halls of residence in my pyjamas, writing an essay, I heard a faint knock on the door. When I opened it, Emma, a usually glamorous, very attractive, and outgoing friend from across the corridor, was standing in her pyjamas and dressing gown, holding two coffee mugs and a pack of chocolate biscuits.

"Hi," I said, surprised to see her.

"Hey, am I interrupting?" she asked.

"Nothing that can't wait. Especially for coffee and chocolate," I replied, opening the door further and allowing Emma inside. I cleared my bed, and we sat down. Emma looked a little nervous.

"You okay?" I asked, tearing into the biscuits.

"Yeah, of course," she said, clearly lying.

"Emma." She looked up. "What's on your mind?"

Emma sighed.

"I need some help, and I thought you might be the best person to ask."

"Okay, what do you need help with?"

Emma leaned back against my wall and crossed her legs under her as she held her mug.

"I'm not sure how to say this," she said.

"Say what? Come on. You can do it. I believe in you," I said, smiling.

She looked over at me and blinked. "I need some sex advice," she said, embarrassed.

Let me tell you why I was more than a little surprised. Emma had a sense of humour as crude, if not worse, than mine. She was twenty, like me, and, frankly, stunning. Emma had short bobbed blonde hair and curves where little me wished I had them, and most of the time, she was the life of the party. She'd be out clubbing in barely-there minidresses twice a week and almost always had a guy on her arm. By our age and with her confidence, I assumed she was the last person on campus to need sex advice.

"How can I help?" I replied softly.

"Well, believe it or not, I've only done it a few times and not for over two years."

"That's not a bad thing, Emma," I replied encouragingly.

"Isn't it?" she asked.

"Not at all. What's the problem?"

"I've been seeing Adrian for nearly a month now, and I let him believe I knew what I would be doing when we get to that point, but I haven't really got a clue, and I don't want to look silly."

"Emma, I've met Adrian. He is the type of guy that would understand. I'm surprised you misled him."

"I'd been drinking, and we were kissing in an alleyway in town. Everything was so hot that I didn't want to ruin it, so I delayed things by suggesting an alleyway wasn't the place for our first time together."

"So you lied?" I asked.

"No. He assumed I'd had plenty of experience, so I went along with it."

"But if you have done it before?" I said curiously.

She sighed. "I was seventeen. He was twenty. I didn't know him well, but we hooked up a few times, and one thing led to another. There was no fooling around, really. We never even got naked. We just went

83

to a park at night a few times and did it on the grass in the dark. It kinda put me off, if I'm honest, so I haven't got around to it again."

"Oh. But now you're with Adrian, and you want to?"

"Yes," she said quickly. "Adrian's made me interested in it again."

"I see, so how can I help?" I asked curiously.

"I don't know. I just wanted someone to talk to that won't judge me. You seem nice (I try!), normal (hardly), and I'm guessing you're not a virgin (if only you knew) and that you can keep a secret (I keep my secrets pretty well, which is why you don't know them, Emma)."

"I see. Well, your secret is safe with me, Emma."

"Thanks."

"So, what do you want to do?"

"I have no idea."

I sat there momentarily, studying the Minnie Mouse logos on my pyjamas and picking biscuit crumbs out of my lap, thinking.

"Well, the way I see it, you have a few options," I finally concluded.

"Which are?"

"One - you tell him the truth. I think he can take it."

"Not an option, sorry, it's humiliating," she replied.

"Emma, you have to stop carrying that baggage around with you. It is far from humiliating."

"Still, no," she insisted.

"Two - you don't tell him anything and muddle through."

"Also, not an option. I want us both to enjoy it a lot more than I did the first few times, at least."

"Three - dump him and be honest with the next guy."

"No," she laughed, seeing the funny side.

"Four - Get dressed, go out tonight, pick up a guy in town, and get some practice. I don't recommend that, by the way. It's just a potential solution." She laughed again. I paused.

"Is there a five?" she asked.

"It's a bit off the wall," I replied.

"Try me."

"You find a guy you can trust to help you practise quickly."

She stared at me for a second, then looked down.

"Yeah, that's an option. But it couldn't be anyone at Uni. Adrian would find out. There's someone at home that might help, but home is two hundred miles away, and I'm not going back until the end of term."

Emma looked a little sad. I wanted to help. Then an idea came to me.

"I might know a guy."

Emma looked up quickly. "Really?"

"Really."

"From Uni?"

"Nope."

"Who?"

I took a deep breath. The only people who knew of my previous sexual encounters - the threesome, the foursome, the gangbang, etc. were all friends of my ex, who was at a different university and with whom I was no longer in contact. I'd loved all that but kept it to myself. Too many girls are branded a slut for doing what they want. While I had no shame about my sexual experiences, I also didn't want some opinionated weasel judging me for them. My newest secret was a little more controversial still. Paul, my ex's dad, was also old enough to be my dad. Our little arrangement saw me swanning around his house dressed like a (legal) teenager, then him taking me to bed and keeping me there all afternoon and all night, screwing my brains out.

I wondered how Paul would react to me taking another girl around for him to play with. How he might reward me for providing him with a new pussy to fuck. I also started to get more than a little excited to watch them together, given that Emma was hot, and I'd already discovered that I liked women too.

"Just to be clear," I started, "we're not judging, are we?"

"God, no, I just bared my soul to you."

"And you can keep a secret, Emma?"

"Of course," she said curiously.

"I'm screwing my ex's dad," I blurted out.

She stared at me, her mouth open a little.

"Wait, what?" she said, even more curious.

"The guy I was seeing before I came to Uni cheated on me. His parents got divorced, and his dad and I always liked each other, but nothing happened. I went around to drop my ex's stuff off when I was eighteen, and something nearly did, but we were interrupted. Then I bumped into him again last month and spent the night at his house."

"Doing what?" Emma asked naively.

I raised an eyebrow and smiled.

"Fuck, P. You keep your cards close to your chest. So are you seeing him properly?"

"God, no. My parents wouldn't understand. He's their friend and has been since before I was born. And he's almost thirty years older than me. It's just an arrangement we both like a lot."

"I take it he's hot?"

I picked up my phone and showed Emma a handsome photo of Paul.

"And the sex is something else," I said proudly.

"And you want me to have sex with him?" she asked, still looking shocked.

"It's an idea. Given the chance, he'd be into you - in more ways than one. I'd be there to help, of course."

"Sorry?"

"Well, I could help if you wanted me to."

Emma thought about it for a moment, and I wouldn't push.

"But he's miles away, too, isn't he?"

"I'm going home this weekend. You could always come with me," I said, smiling. "Why don't you think about it and let me know? I can always ask him if he's up for meeting you."

Emma collected the mugs and what was left of the biscuits and stood.

"I will. Think about it, I mean. When do you need to know?"

"Tomorrow lunchtime, so I can get my mum to make up the spare room for Friday night. I can easily explain our absence overnight on Saturday if you come. I'll say we're going clubbing or something," I said, encouragingly, but not too encouragingly.

As she left my room, I saw cogs whirring in Emma's mind. I set about re-starting my essay, and a few minutes later, the door knocked again.

Emma stood there, looking nervous but excited. "I'm in," she said hesitantly.

"You're sure?" I asked, giving her a chance to change her mind.

"I'm sure," she replied.

"Send me a hot pic of you, will you? But not in a club dress. Something a bit more girl-next-door if you have one. I'll send it to Paul."

She smiled, "I have just the photo."

Moments later, Emma sent me a lovely photo of her in a little pair of cute white shorts and an equally cute baby blue blouse. It looked professionally taken, but then she was an aspiring model, so it probably was. I gave up on my essay and called Paul.

"Hi," he said, answering quickly. "Still coming for a cuppa this weekend?"

"Of course," I said sweetly, "but I need to ask you something."

"Anything."

"Mind if I bring someone?" I asked.

"Who?"

"Her name's Emma. She's a friend from University who needs our help. If you fancy it?"

"Help how?" he asked curiously.

"She's inexperienced. She is not a virgin, but it's been a while. She's not done much else and wants to know what she's doing when she has sex with her new boyfriend for the first time."

"Are you serious?"

"Very. And she's hot."

"Am I hearing this correctly, or am I dreaming?" he laughed.

"No, you're hearing correctly. Two for the price of one this weekend, if you can handle two of us?"

"As if you need to ask," he replied excitedly.

"Fab, I'll send you a pic of her. See you around two on Saturday?"

"See you then."

He hung up, and I sent him the photo. It took him a minute. Then I received a response.

'Bring her!'

Emma and I packed for the weekend at my parent's house the following day, then went to lectures. At lunchtime, we collected our cases and headed to the train station. It was only an hour or so to my home, and we were due to go to Pauls on Saturday afternoon, but Emma was already visibly nervous.

Given that the train was mostly empty, I filled her in on the details.

"He calls me Pixie or Pix," I said, staring out the train window as we hurtled through the countryside.

"Why?" Emma asked.

"When I was seeing his son, I went through a phase of trying to look innocent. I always wore little summer dresses, perfect hair, and little make-up. It turned my ex on. It turns out it turned his dad on too. He once referred to me as a little Pixie floating around the house, and it stuck. Now it's his name for me."

"So he likes the sweet and innocent look?"

"Yeah, that's why I knew he'd like you. You're beautiful in everything you wear and do an excellent girl-next-door. "

Emma blushed. My compliment landed in a way I didn't expect. I didn't want to confuse the weekend by letting her know I couldn't wait to see her naked, and she didn't yet know I had a thing for girls, but she responded to my comment. So maybe...

"And he'll be gentle?" she asked.

"With you, yes."

"And with you?"

"No," I replied, biting my lip, becoming horny at the mere thought.

"Oh," she replied.

"And it's a safe space, Em. It would be best if you took the opportunity to try anything and everything you are curious about. We won't judge, either of us."

Her eyes sparkled a little, clearly getting more excited as the train drew closer to my family home.

After we arrived, we had dinner with my parents, then went to a local pub so I could introduce Emma to a few of my friends from home. No surprise that the beautiful stranger attracted a lot of attention, and if she'd wanted to, she could have had her pick of the guys and some of the girls in the place.

The following morning, my mum went to tennis, my dad disappeared to golf, and Emma and I bathed and pampered ourselves, ready for our trip to Paul's.

Emma's nerves returned occasionally, but I was entertaining enough to keep her mostly distracted. Being the same dress size as me, I ironed two of my short white Pixie dresses, one for each of us. Mine was a little less reserved and far too short to wear in public. It also had slits up the side to make matters worse or better, depending on your perspective. Emma's was also very short, but nothing shorter than the barely-there dresses she was often comfortable to wear to a nightclub.

I folded them and put them into my rucksack with a few overnight things, Emma packed her bag, and after lunch, we set out on the short walk to Paul's house in the afternoon sun.

As we approached, Emma became really nervous.

"I don't think I can do this," she said, stopping dead in the street and refusing to move.

"Look, Em. There's no expectation on you. You can do anything or nothing, honestly. Why don't you come inside and meet Paul, have a cuppa, and we can leave if you're not into it? He'll understand."

"Okay," she said, uncharacteristically timidly.

We walked up his driveway, and I knocked on the door. He opened it, smiling warmly.

"Hey, Pixie," he said. "I see you've brought a friend."

"Hey," I said, fluttering my eyes at him. "This is Emma."

Emma looked up and smiled, relaxing a little now, having finally laid eyes on him. She seemed impressed. We stepped inside, dropped our bags on the sofa, followed him to the kitchen and stood together while Paul made us drinks.

"So, Emma, my little Pixie tells me you'd like our help?" he said with his back to us.

"Err, yeah," she said happily, clearly not phased by Paul's age compared to ours.

He turned and took her mug to her, looking into her eyes. "Pixie was right. You really are beautiful," he said.

As I watched Emma's reaction, I knew she would have a good night. She fluttered her eyelashes at him and looked down, embarrassed.

"Thanks," she said sheepishly, clearly under his spell. I knew how that felt and what it would mean for her in the bedroom.

He turned his attention to me. "Hey," he said, stepping forward.

"Hey," I replied softly as he touched my hip and kissed me. I reached up and pulled him in, our tongues dancing together as we kissed.

Eventually, I let him withdraw and looked across at Emma, standing beside me, eyes wide.

"Don't forget Emma," I told Paul while not breaking eye contact with her. She bit her bottom lip and looked up at him, evidently into my suggestion. Paul held my hand as he stepped over to her and put his hand behind her neck. She tilted her head back, and he leaned in. I watched excitedly as their tongues explored each other's mouths for the first time. Emma reached out, put a hand on his hip, and pulled him closer. He leaned against her slight body, pressing her against the kitchen worktop as they enjoyed each other. Eventually, they relaxed. Paul stepped back and went to collect my mug. Emma looked across at me with her eyes sparkling and mouthed, "Wow".

Nobody's mind was on our drinks right now.

"Why don't Em and I change while our drinks cool?" I suggested.

"Both changing?" Paul asked, surprised. "Two Pixies?"

Emma found her confidence. "There's only one Pixie," she said, smiling at me, then turned to look at him, "I'll be your nymph."

I took Emma's hand and led her back into the living room to collect our bags. Then we went up to his bedroom to change. I passed Emma her dress, then removed my shoes, jeans, and bra. I slipped my tiny white dress over my head and turned to look at Emma, who was in her lingerie, just about to put on her dress. She looked across at me.

"No bra?" she asked.

"No need, no point," I said seductively. Emma smiled at me, unclipped her bra, and let it fall, dropping it into her rucksack. I studied her almost naked body subtly. I decided right then that if I had the chance, I would enjoy her.

She slipped on her dress and looked at me. "Will I do?" she asked sweetly, giving me a twirl.

"Stunning," I replied.

She watched as I lifted my dress slightly, put my thumbs into the waistband of my thong and removed it. She looked across at me, seeing me in a new, sexual, confident light. Seeing me like that helped her confidence.

"You don't have to, but he likes me to be available whenever he wants," I said.

She blinked. "In for a penny," she whispered, removing her black lace thong and dropping it in her bag.

We brushed our hair and stowed our bags out of the way.

"Wait," Emma said, grabbing her phone. She leaned into me as she lifted her arm high, and we looked up. Then Emma took a selfie of us leaning into each other in our short dresses. She showed it to me; we did look hot, I thought. We strolled back to the kitchen barefoot, in only our little white dresses. We walked in hand-in-hand as Paul looked up from his mug. "Wow. You both look..."

"-fuckable?" I interrupted, teasing.

"I was going with beautiful, but both work."

I gently nudged Emma forward a little into some space and encouraged her to twirl. It's incredible how quickly Paul's new Nymph got into character, spinning on her toes, letting her dress rise just enough for him to realise that she was naked under her dress.

"I think we'll have some fun with Nymph tonight, Pix."

Emma looked at me, a little flustered. "We?" she asked.

I looked at her, a little embarrassed.

"You haven't told her, have you, Pixie?" Paul said.

I looked at the floor. "I thought she was committing to enough tonight without that," I said softly.

"Without what?" Emma said sweetly, stepping towards me, recognising my insecurity.

"Pixie fancies you," Paul said, saving me the job of telling her myself.

"Really?" Emma asked softly, taking my hand.

I looked up nervously at Emma's face.

"You never told me you were bi," she said, lifting a hand and running her fingers through my long brown hair.

"As I said, I thought you had enough to contend with this weekend without me throwing myself at you," I said, wishing Paul hadn't brought it up.

"You can throw yourself at me any time you want, Pixie," Emma whispered.

I looked up, startled. "Wait, what?"

"Let's just say my lack of experience only extends to men," she replied.

We looked into each other's eyes.

"I sense a kiss coming on," Paul said, excited at the thought.

Emma leaned forward and kissed me. She was the first woman I'd kissed since my encounters with Jane, my ex's friend's girlfriend, almost two years before. I'd forgotten how much I enjoyed a woman's kiss. Emma was passionate, her tongue exploring my mouth deeply while I explored hers. She pulled our bodies together, and for a moment, we completely forgot Paul was watching us enjoying each other. Eventually, reluctantly, we stepped away, staring into each other's eyes affectionately.

"Finish your drinks, ladies. We have more exciting things to do."

His voice distracted us, and we all finished our lukewarm drinks quickly. Paul stepped between us and kissed us both, one at a time. Then he led the way as his Pixie and Nymph followed him to his bedroom.

As we entered, I turned to Emma while Paul sat on the bed, watching. I slowly undid the buttons on the front of her dress, allowing it to fall open, revealing her freshly shaven pussy to me for the first time. I didn't touch her, nor did I remove the dress, knowing that from where Paul was sitting, side-on to both of us, he couldn't see as much of her beautiful body as I could, which must have been driving him wild.

She smiled at me and reached up, slowly opening my dress, button by button, as she stared into my eyes. When she had finished, I peeled the dress off my shoulders and let it fall to the floor, then took her hand and turned her to face Paul as I stood behind her. I put my hands on her hips, and she wriggled happily as I slid them up the side of her body. I looked across at Paul as I peeled back her dress, and it fell.

His eyes had a fire in them as he looked at Emma, facing him naked as I stood behind her, looking over her shoulder with my hands back on her hips. I whispered in her ear. "I'm here if you need me."

"Be gentle with her," I said to Paul. "The first time around, at least."

He raised a hand, and Emma stepped away from me slowly, walking towards him. She took his hand, and he gently pulled her close. I walked over and sat in a chair in the corner of Paul's bedroom and crossed my legs seductively, he glanced over to me, and I nodded to him, and then his attention returned to Emma. I sat back, watching and waiting until they needed me.

He looked into her eyes. "Do you want to just get it over with, or do you want the Pixie treatment?" he asked softly. "You must be nervous."

"I want what she wants," Emma replied, tilting her head toward me. "When I can handle it."

"We'll have to work up to it," he said.

"We have all night, don't we?" she said sweetly.

"We do," he replied.

I watched silently as he stood before her and took off his T-Shirt. She reached up instinctively and touched his chest. He was patient and gave her a moment before reaching for his belt. She seemed to want to get involved and reached out to help him. He withdrew his hands, and she undid his belt and the buttons on the front of his jeans. He pushed his jeans to the floor and stepped out of them. He looked good, standing in black satin boxers in front of her. She seemed to think so, too, as she stepped forward, and he kissed her. As my lover seduced my friend, I watched patiently, absently drawing patterns on my collarbone with my fingernail. She raised a hand and placed it on his growing cock through his boxers. So far, she seemed comfortable and knew what she was doing. I hadn't asked her how much she'd done, so for all I knew, she'd never seen a cock up close before in the daylight, let alone had one in her mouth. She was about to experience both.

She eventually slid her hand inside his boxers. I felt myself getting hornier by the second as her dainty wrist slid up and down inside them slowly. Paul stopped kissing her briefly and whispered something to her. She nodded, and he removed his boxers. She looked down at his cock, then glanced across at me, looking a little nervous.

That was my cue. Paul climbed onto the bed and lay in the middle of it, and I went over and stood with my arm around Emma.

"Have you given a blow job before?" I asked.

"No!" she whispered.

"Well, you're about to," I whispered back. You climb on there and kneel next to Paul. I'm going around the other side,"

Emma took instruction well, and by the time I'd slid onto the bed on the opposite side, with Paul between us, she was sitting on her ankles, looking down at his cock.

"Hey," I said to Paul, sliding my hand down his chest and taking his cock. "Mind if I use you as a teaching aid?"

"Be my guest," he said, putting his hands behind his head and looking forward to having his cock sucked by two young women.

I looked across at Emma. "Want a demo?" She nodded.

I smiled at her as I leaned forward and circled the tip of Paul's cock with my tongue, then took him into my mouth, flicking my tongue over the tip inside my mouth before taking him deep and bobbing up and down gently. I reminded myself that despite being horny and wanting Paul inside me, deep-throating him in front of Emma would probably do more harm than good at this point. I gave him, by my standards, vanilla oral for a few moments, then sat up.

"Your turn," I said to Emma, licking my lips.

She was horny, having watched me suck the cock she planned on having between her legs later. She wasted no time in leaning forward and sucking him. Paul understood the teaching process and started to moan his encouragement as she bobbed up and down. I'm convinced I heard the occasional gag from Emma - but I may have been wrong. She was eager and didn't come up for air for ages. When she eventually did, she looked at Paul.

"You're a natural," he said warmly. "You can come here with Pixie and practice on me whenever you want."

She smiled, pleased with herself, and immediately bent back down and returned to her new favourite activity, surprising us both. I watched as she became more and more confident, adding hands to the mix and licking his shaft and balls. Paul was right. She was a natural.

"Em," I said softly.

"Hey, earth to Em," I said.

She managed a muffled moan, acknowledging my calls.

"You have other things to be doing. Paul will come in your mouth later if you want him to."

She slowly withdrew her mouth from him, and Paul sighed happily.

"Lie down," I whispered to her. She looked nervous again but lay beside Paul, who rolled onto his side to face her. He used a deep lingering kiss to distract her as he slid his hand down her neck, across her nipples and towards her clit. There was no resistance. Before he'd even touched it, she opened her legs slightly. I shuffled around on the bed a little to get a better view. Her pussy looked perfect. She'd shaven completely, and her small, perfectly formed pink mound caught the eye. I wanted to taste her so badly. But this wasn't about me, not yet anyway.

Paul slid a finger to her clit, and she moaned loudly.

"Has anyone done this before?" Paul asked.

"Yes, but not a guy for a long time," she managed through her moans, reaching up and pulling his mouth back onto hers. Paul continued pleasuring her for a minute or two. I watched as he slowly slid his finger down and penetrated her with it gradually.

Emma panted and moaned softly, clearly loving Paul's attention, and lifted her legs a little, opening them wider.

I looked down and realised that I'd subconsciously parted my knees and started rubbing my clit while I watched them. I smiled as I continued, enjoying the slow sensual show before me.

"Can I taste you?" I heard Paul ask. She didn't respond. She just released his neck and put her arms by her side. Paul kissed her neck, then her nipples, then slid down between her legs and, as he did the first time he went down on me, kissed her clit gently to judge her reaction. Her reaction was the same as mine had been.

"Fuck," she whispered, arching her back. Paul smiled, and I watched his face disappear between her pale white legs.

I continued masturbating, watching Emma writhe on the bed in pleasure as Paul lavished his attention on her pussy. I would be horny, wet, and ready for my turn when it eventually came. But this part of the afternoon wasn't about me, and I knew it.

Paul started to slow and ran his tongue up her body as she wriggled in ecstasy.

I reached for the box of condoms on the bedside table, took one out, and put it on the bed next to him as he returned to lie beside her.

"Ready?" he whispered.

"Ready," she replied with impressive confidence.

"That's my cue to leave," I said.

Paul didn't respond, he knew, but Emma looked over.

"You're going?" she asked as Paul reached for the condom packet and opened it.

"Just for a little while. It would be best if you experienced this without me. I'll be back," I said, stroking Emma's leg briefly and kissing Paul on the cheek. "Enjoy."

Paul rolled on the condom and looked at her. She bit her bottom lip and opened her legs again. I slipped off the bed and wandered over to the door as he took position between them.

97

Emma looked at him as I turned away and heard her inhale loudly as if experiencing penetration properly for the first time. I remember that moment well. It was in this very house, but not with Paul.

I left the door open and went and sat on his son's - my ex-boyfriend's - bed. The bed I'd lost my virginity on three years before. I lay back, naked, listening as my friend lost hers - metaphorically, though not actually physically, with his father. Losing her virginity while fumbling around in a park all those years ago served to help her today.

It was all too familiar - the 'oooh's and 'aahs' and gentle whimpers in the first few minutes as Emma's body adjusted to being penetrated for the first time in years. I winced as I lay on the bed, remembering the pain of losing my virginity despite my boyfriend's patience. I was confident that his father was showing Emma the same gentle kindness. Thankfully she'd been here before, albeit not as romantically or erotically. I hoped she wasn't experiencing quite as much discomfort as a result. After a few moments, Emma's whimpers changed to moans. She was beginning to really enjoy Paul making love to her. Moments later, she became louder.

It was getting too much for me, and I slid my hand down my body and against my clit, imagining Paul slowly driving his cock into Emma, opening up her body to a world of sexual experiences she could only yet imagine. I fingered myself, and as Emma became louder still, and I could hear Paul grunting and preparing to come, I had a massive orgasm on my ex-boyfriend's bed. More extensive than any I had achieved in it before, that's for sure. I raised my pelvis, coming hard as I heard the now familiar sound of Paul reaching his climax and Emma moaning as he did so.

I lay there for a few minutes, listening to the faint sounds of talking and Emma giggling. I heard a door close, so I got up and returned to Paul's bedroom. He was lying on his bed, still naked and looking hot. I wandered over to him as I heard running water and the sound of Emma singing in the shower coming from his ensuite.

"Hey," I said, sliding onto the bed beside him.

"Hey, Pix," he replied, putting an arm around me as I lay with him.

"She sounds happy. How is she?" I asked.

"Fine. More than fine, actually. She seems a very happy little nymph. Judging by the look in her eyes, she's hooked."

"And how was she?" I whispered in his ear seductively.

He looked at me, fire dancing in his eyes. I didn't need him to answer. I'd bought him a beautiful twenty-year-old model who had willingly offered her body to him. I smiled. "I'm sure you can find a way to thank me for her later," I said as his attention returned to me. He looked at me in a way that told me his gratitude would most likely make me scream. I smiled and bit my bottom lip, keen to find out.

I heard the shower turn off, and a few moments later, a newly confident and very happy Emma emerged from the ensuite wearing nothing but a smile. She wandered over to the bed where we lay, climbed on opposite me and lay on Paul's shoulder, looking into my eyes.

"Hey," she said sweetly.

"Hey," I replied, "how are you, or do I not need to ask?"

She smiled, then looked the tiniest bit embarrassed.

"Have you got anything we can use to celebrate Nymph's real first time?" I whispered to Paul.

"No, but I bet you two want to catch up, so I can always nip out and get us all something." I smiled at him and slid my leg across his body, brushing my thigh against his soft cock. "Thanks," I whispered.

Emma and I sat up to release him, and he quickly dressed and headed out the door, casting a naughty look at his Pixie and his Nymph, sitting naked on his bed as he disappeared. We lay back down, facing each other, waiting for the sound of the front door closing. Click.

"So? How was It?" I asked.

Emma rolled onto her back, put her hand on her tummy and giggled.

"Fucking fantastic, P. I don't know how it can get better than that!"

I smiled. "Oh, Emma, it most certainly can." Emma went all girly on me. "Do you reckon he'll want to make love to me again later?" she asked dreamily.

"No," I said softly. She looked at me, startled for a second. I blinked. "You told him you want what I want."

"So?"

"So, assuming you're up for it, next time, he's going to fuck you."

"What's the difference?" she asked excitedly.

I melted at the thought of Paul inside me. She saw it. I leaned forward and kissed her just briefly.

"Wait and see. You've only just started, and we've got nearly twenty-four more hours here with him yet."

Paul returned with four bottles of Prosecco to keep us girls fuelled for the night and a case of lager for himself. We were still giggling and chatting naked on his bed when he reappeared in the bedroom carrying a tray with two glasses of fizz for us, the open bottle, and a lager for himself.

I could tell by the looks he gave us that he thought he was dreaming. Men his age usually pay significant sums of money to have two attractive twenty-year-olds naked in their beds. On the other hand, Paul had my body on tap regularly, and this weekend I even bought a model with me for him to enjoy.

I wasn't much less dreamy if I'm honest. I was always horny and available for Paul from the second I walked through his front door. I was like a cat in heat, happy and often desperate to open my legs, my mouth, or my ass for him at a moment's notice. This weekend, with the beautiful Emma swanning around naked, who was already showing signs of being entirely sexually open-minded, I was obscenely horny—made worse by the fact that since we got to Paul's house, we had discovered that we were both into Paul and Emma and I were also into each other.

We had chatted briefly while he was gone. Emma was open to exploring more with Paul. Still, rather than anything else being an event (given the "event" she had already been part of this afternoon), she wanted things to be a little more naturally occurring. It worked for me, but I was a little concerned. If Paul and I got up to our usual bedroom antics - which I hoped we would considering how horny I was - Emma was going to go from gentle vanilla blowjobs and passionate lovemaking to witnessing deepthroat, rough sex, and probably anal too. On that basis, I suddenly became the one who was a little self-conscious. She seemed open-minded, but she'd see me in a new light, and if she disapproved, I risked my whole halls of residence finding out what I like to do behind closed doors.

Then I thought about it. The most glamorous, attractive, and desired girl on campus had approached me to help her gain sexual experience. Then she came along to my - I don't know what Paul is, let's call him a fuck-buddy - she came along to my fuck-buddy's house, got naked, watched me suck his cock, sucked him herself, then opened her legs and invited a guy old enough to be her father to have sex with her. What was I worried about? - She would hardly share that with the world, especially as an aspiring model with a vast social media following.

I relaxed as Paul passed me, then Emma, a glass of Prosecco. We sat gracefully, knees bent, legs to our side, with our ankles together, fulfilling the brief of being a pixie and a nymph on his bed. We took sips politely, then smiled at each other and finished the drinks quickly. Student life can do that to a girl.

Emma took my glass and put it with hers on Paul's bedside table, then looked at me sweetly. She shuffled over, brimming with confidence, and kissed me briefly. I swooned. Her kisses were soft, sensual, and erotic. She wanted to explore my mouth as I did hers. She lifted a hand to my cheek, then turned to Paul, who was standing fully dressed, holding a bottle of lager while watching us quietly.

"Mind if I borrow Pixie for a while?" she asked, smiling at him. My heart fluttered.

"Mind if I watch?" Paul asked.

Emma nodded to the chair in the corner of his bedroom, where I had sat, watching them together. "Take a seat." Paul wandered over and sat down.

She turned to look at me. "You've done this before, right?" she whispered.

"A couple of times, a while ago," I replied sheepishly.

"Well, this is something I have a little more experience in. Why don't I drive?" Emma replied, staring into my eyes.

"Okay," I whispered.

She leaned forward and kissed me again, more deeply but equally sensually, tucking my long brown hair behind my ear and tracing her fingertip down my neck, across my shoulder, and then down the outside of my arm. Words cannot describe the feeling Emma was giving me. And I think she knew it.

She lifted my arms, and I willingly moved as she positioned me gently in the middle of the bed, then continued kissing me as she knelt over me and slowly pushed me back onto the pillows. She put her arms on either side of my head as her tongue slowly explored every part of my mouth. Then she lowered her body slowly onto mine. I felt our nipples touch - the contact sending a pleasurable shiver down my spine, and then her body pressed against me. I opened my legs and bent my knees as her pelvis settled against mine between them, the warmth of her soft skin against me. I needed to breathe. Reluctantly, I turned away from her, ending the lingering kiss. Emma was in no mood to let anything end there. My exposed neck became her next target as she leaned down, traced her tongue behind my ear, and slowly kissed and licked down my shoulders. I began to moan, desperate for more.

I arched my back a little, pressing my chest into the air. She lifted and looked up at me, smiling, her intent clear. She looked at me, slid downward just a little, and stared into my eyes as she flicked her tongue over my nipple. I sighed. She sucked on it gently, making me wild with desire, then drew a straight line across my chest with her tongue and started on the other, slowly flicking, licking and sucking it until both nipples stood to attention for her. She reached up and cupped my breasts, massing them as she kissed my stomach, then slid slowly downward.

My last (and first) female sexual partner was attractive, but Emma was simply beautiful. She had piercing blue eyes, beautiful straight blonde bobbed blonde hair, and a smile that could melt ice. The day we met, I had sexual thoughts about her, but I never dreamed in a million years that one day she would be naked and on top of me. I wanted to record everything in my mind, just in case it never happened again.

By now, Emma was kissing my inner thigh, close enough but far enough away to tease me beyond my wildest dreams. Yes, I'd given myself an orgasm earlier while she had sex with Paul, but that wasn't nearly enough, given the day we were all having.

She stopped and looked up at me as I panted, wanting to grab her head and pull her in.

"We've been living ten feet from each other for five months. Don't you wish we'd done this sooner?" Emma asked, smiling cheekily.

I was about to reply as I looked down at her beautiful face between my legs, but as I started to form the words, I felt her warm, soft tongue against my clit.

"Oh my God," was all I could manage as Emma set to work on my pussy.

She was true to her word and was no amateur. She knew exactly where the most sensitive areas were and wasted little time teasing each of them. She moaned softly as she slid further down, lapping against my opening before sliding her tongue between my lips and inside my body. I was in heaven. I lay there as she passionately and attentively explored me, but I still wanted more. I wanted to taste her too. To taste the girl I'd been secretly admiring for months. I lifted my head, and she looked up at me.

"Any soreness from earlier?" I whispered, not wanting to hurt her in any way.

"None at all," she said, smiling.

I sat up and encouraged Emma to lie on her side. I slipped down beside her, head to toe, then slowly licked upward from just above her knee, and she parted her legs as I arrived at my destination. She giggled as I licked my fingers and then placed them on her clit gently. I looked down at my body to see her lying on her side, looking longingly at my legs. Her face was just inches away, I opened them, and I saw her smile as she tilted her head forward and used her tongue on my body once more.

I could wait no longer. I removed my fingers and pressed my tongue against Emma's clit, then started drawing circles around it as her body reacted, and she began to moan sweetly. I leaned forwards, pressing my head deeper between her legs, and reached my goal, slipping my tongue inside her and tasting her juices for the very first time. She tasted every bit as good as she looked.

I felt her pull at my hip and instinctively knew what she craved. I lifted my leg over her head and settled my pussy over her face as she rolled onto her back and pulled her legs open wider, encouraging me to continue. I struggled to cope with her attention, a stirring inside my body growing. Then, suddenly, things got a little out of hand, in a good way.

I felt a hand stroke down my back. A masculine hand that couldn't be my sweet Emma. I looked up from her pussy, my lips glistening with her juices, as Paul stood before me, now naked and holding his rock-hard cock. Emma also noticed him. She reached out and stroked his leg, acknowledging his welcome interruption.

"I've got something here Pixie needs," he said. He was right.

I climbed off Emma and lay on my back, my ass on the edge of the bed, as Paul grabbed my ankles, straightened my legs and spread them wide.

I reached down and guided his cock to my pussy. How easily he slid his cock inside me made clear how horny I was.

"Fucking hell, Pix, you're wet," he said, feeling my warmth enveloping his cock.

"So's Nymph," I panted as I adjusted to his presence. We both looked across at her, kneeling and watching excitedly.

"Want to see how Pix likes it?" Paul asked her.

"God, yes," she said, bouncing on the bed a little.

Paul withdrew, then pressed my legs wide and slammed his cock into me, making me howl in ecstasy.

"Fucking hell," Emma said, smiling.

I looked up at her as Paul withdrew again, biting my lip as he started to thrust deeply and vigorously inside me. I whimpered and moaned, even more turned on than usual, in the knowledge that Emma was watching my body taking a pounding from Paul's cock. Her eyes glistened. The sight of me enjoying his relentless thrusting turned her on. She wanted it too. Between my moans, I managed to speak.

"Do you want Paul to fuck you like this later, Nymph?" I panted.

She looked at him, studying the carnal desire in his eyes as he continued enjoying me. She looked down between my legs, watching his glistening cock disappear deep inside my body over and over. Then she looked into my eyes, wide and dancing wildly as Paul drove me to orgasmic bliss.

"Yes," she said. "Yes, please."

That was all I needed to tip me over the edge. The thought of watching Paul take her like this, added to the fact that he was already doing it to me, made an orgasm grow inside my body quickly. I reached out and pressed my hand between Emma's legs as she knelt beside me. She separated them quickly, allowing me to rub her clit. I was rough with her, testing her desire to experience Paul as his carnal best. Her response was perfect, throwing her head back and leaning back onto her hands as I pleasured her. I slid my other hand to my clit, intent on coming hard on Paul's cock. He saw it all, and it affected him too. He started to grunt as his girls moaned loudly, and I felt him begin to tense. Emma's body began to shake. I didn't realise how horny she really was until her legs gave way and slipped sideways, and she ground her pelvis onto my hand, coming hard on my trapped fingers. It pushed me over the edge, and I removed my other hand from my clit and ran my hands through my hair as I started to shake myself, my legs quivering as Paul still held my ankles in the air.

"Come in me, baby. Fill me," I begged.

Paul let go of my ankles, slid his hands behind my knees, and pressed my legs onto my chest. Emma looked up from her orgasm, eagerly watching as Paul groaned loudly and emptied his seed inside my Pussy. He pushed my tiny body down deep into the mattress aggressively as his carnal urge to breed me led him to force my pussy to take every last drop.

I lay there panting, lost in orgasmic ecstasy, then remembered to check on Emma. As she sat there, still gently massaging her clit against my fingers, the look on her beautiful face told us everything Paul and I needed to know. Emma was now officially Nymph. And she was ready and willing to do anything.

Paul withdrew his cock, making me moan a little, then let go of my legs, gently helping me shuffle up onto the bed next to Emma as she released my hand from beneath her. As he wandered off to the bathroom, she watched him longingly.

"God, I want to try that," she said.

"You will later," I assured her. "There's lots to try yet."

Paul came out of the bathroom, sitting on the bed beside us. He kissed Emma passionately while I watched, then leaned down and kissed me.

"It's like all of your Christmases have come at once, right?" I teased as he sat back up.

He smiled. "And to think I have you both all night still," he replied. "It's nearly dinner time. Why don't you two drink more Prosecco, and I'll pop out and get us takeaway to keep our energy up?"

"Well, you should. You do have two women to satisfy tonight," Emma said. I giggled, seeing myself in her and liking her more by the minute.

Paul dressed and headed downstairs while I took a quick shower, and Emma slipped back into her dress. When I came out of the shower, I did the same. We finished the first bottle of prosecco quickly in Paul's bedroom. Then we went downstairs just after he left to go to the takeaway to open another. We were becoming light-headed, giggly, and very honest. The relentless physical contact between Emma and me, holding hands, cuddling and the occasional kiss, added an air of affection to the eroticism. I studied Emma as she made her way through another glass of Prosecco, wondering how she was really feeling.

"Em, you okay, you know, with all this?" I asked.

She put down her glass and looked at me. "I'm more than okay," she said confidently. "P, you are a goddess—my heroine. To think I came to you for advice because I thought you probably had a completely normal sex life. You hide it very well," she said, smiling.

"People judge," I replied.

"Fuck them. Not literally, you know," Emma said, laughing. She put her glass down and looked me in the eye.

"So, while we're alone, what am I in for later, besides your sexy older man fucking me to kingdom come?" she asked.

"Depends," I replied casually.

"On what?"

"How much do you want to try?"

"Well, not wanting to sound like a prude, but how much more can there possibly be?"

"I love it when I make a guy come in my mouth or throat."

"Throat?" she asked curiously.

"Deepthroat. It's a technique. Men love it,"

"Okay, do you swallow it?"

"Always! Good girls do!" I said, fluttering my eyelashes at her. She smiled.

"Noted, and?"

"It takes some patience first, but anal is amazing." Emma picked up her drink and finished it quickly, then screwed up her nose.

"I don't think..."

"-Don't knock it until you have tried it, sweetie. Not that you have to, of course," I interrupted.

"Does he, you know, finish in there too?"

"Yes, of course, I let him come wherever he wants, as often as he wants."

Emma wasn't disgusted, thankfully, but was a little reserved on the subject.

"Well, in any case, if he's as horny as he usually is, you will see him do it to me at some point after dinner. Then you can let us know what you think."

That ticked Emma's boxes. Regardless of what we were up to, the thought of watching me with Paul turned her on immensely.

"Anything else?" she asked.

"Well, knowing Paul, he'll have some ideas since there are two of us with him tonight. There might be some new things he suggests for both of us. Oh, and don't be surprised if he wants to fuck you in a dozen positions before morning. He likes anything that lets him get in deep. As do I," I said, smiling.

Emma sat back, thinking. Then smiled to herself and looked up. "Well, if this afternoon is anything to go by, count me in."

"Good, because I didn't get to watch him make love to you earlier, so I really want to watch him *fuck* you later."

"Oh, you will," she said sweetly, reaching her hand across the table and holding mine.

The door clicked, and Paul walked in. I looked up at him sweetly.

"Nymph's right. I think you are going to need your energy tonight."

As we sat in Paul's kitchen, eating our dinner and Emma and I making our way through far too much Prosecco, Paul relished happily in having two girls, flirting with each other, and him, wearing my short "Pixie" dresses. Emma watched as I stood up and leaned over the table, pretending to be reaching for noodles, exposing my ass to him. She smiled as he instantly slid his fingers up the inside of my legs and inside my pussy, taking my breath away as I gripped the table for a moment, happily moaning until he removed them. Then I watched Emma go to the fridge beside Paul as he stacked the dishes, claiming to be collecting a bottle of Prosecco, bending at the waist and exposing her pussy. I, too, smiled as he slid his fingers over her ass and teased her sweet pussy lips, taking her breath away.

After we had finished dinner, with Emma and me and more than a little drunk and horny, I decided it was time to move the action back upstairs. We were sitting, looking at each other with anticipation, when Emma came up with a brilliant suggestion.

"Pixie wants to show me how to deepthroat," she said, smiling at Paul. If she hadn't already got his attention, she immediately did.

"Do you now?" he asked, looking across at me.

"And Nymph wants to know what a mouth full of your come tastes like," I replied, turning the focus back to Emma.

"And I bet Paul would love to know how it feels to have Pixie and Nymph working his cock with their mouths simultaneously," she added.

We both turned to Paul. "Or we could watch TV," Emma said, teasing.

"I guess we'd better take this upstairs then," Paul said.

Emma and I stood up and held each other, passionately kissing while Paul retrieved the tray and put some snacks, our drinks, and a few bottles of lager on it, and then we followed him up the stairs. He had yet to get the tray on the table before Emma, and I removed our dresses.

I let Emma lead as Paul stood, and she knelt before him, quickly removing his jeans as he removed his T-shirt. He stood naked, his soft cock hanging in front of her face.

She turned to her side and glanced across at me as she stooped under it and opened her mouth, licking his tip and kissing it slowly, teasingly. She had no intention of taking him in her mouth yet, and it drove him wild.

"She's naughty," he said, sighing at her gentle tongue massage.

"We like naughty," I replied. "We like naughty a lot."

Emma giggled as I walked over to them and knelt opposite her. She slid up the opposite side of Paul's cock, gently kissing his length as it started to swell for her. I leaned in and kissed the other side, and we both looked up at him as we continued. We tracked his cock as it grew hard, arching our necks to keep our mouths perfectly opposite each other as we gently caressed his shaft with our tongues, patiently awaiting his full, impressive erection. It didn't take long.

We didn't speak to each other, but simultaneously Emma and I got up, kissed in front of him, and then walked hand in hand over to his bed. We both knelt in the same places we had been in earlier when I taught Emma how to give her first blow job, waiting for him. He took a swig from his beer bottle and climbed onto the bed between us, rolling onto his back and opening his legs slightly.

Emma couldn't help herself and was down on him quickly, her beautiful blonde hair swishing around her face as she bobbed her mouth up and down on Paul's cock. I watched her work him eagerly.

She was a girl after my own heart and a great candidate for deepthroat training if I could slow her down and let Paul last long enough for her to try it.

I softly stroked her back, ran my hand down her ass, and gently squeezed it. She giggled and sat up.

"Show me," she said eagerly.

"It's just about your gag reflex. You will gag as any cock goes into your throat, but you just learn to control it. Like this," I said. I turned a little, adjusting my position to give me the best chance of taking all of him, then leaned down and blinked at the man with sparkling eyes as I took him into my mouth. I started shallow for a second or two, then closed my eyes as I pressed his cock against my throat. I always gagged at the first attempt, and today was no different. Then I withdrew for a second, took a deep breath, and pushed my face down onto his length, feeling it slide into my throat fully. I held it there for a second, then slid Paul's erection up and down my throat a little before withdrawing.

I heard Emma gasp. I looked up. It wasn't a gasp of horror.

"Wanna try?" I asked sweetly. Emma blinked and leaned down to take him in her mouth.

Now, I have to be honest. As much as I'm a bit of a deepthroat pro (if I do say so myself!), it took a lot of practice. A lot of practice. I learned I could do it quickly, granted, but to handle a cock easily and comfortably, especially a cock the size of Paul's, took quite a while. I know Emma was horny beyond words. And I know she'd had quite a lot to drink. Her immediate ability, however, was mind-blowing.

I watched as she gagged, withdrew, gagged again, and withdrew. Her determination alone was impressive. But after her third attempt, I watched her cute little throat swell as she pushed Paul past the barrier and deep into her. Did she pull off quickly? No, no, she didn't. She held him there and moaned a little, then withdrew enough to catch her breath and pushed him in again. I was as impressed as I was astonished.

I looked up at Paul, who was stunned and ecstatic.

"She really is a natural," I said. Emma withdrew and giggled as she sat up and wiped her mouth.

"Okay?" I asked.

"Very," she replied.

"Fancy something a bit more... ...intense?"

"Bring it on," she said eagerly.

Well, who was I to refuse? "On your feet, sexy," I said to Paul, who knew exactly where I was going next. He climbed off the bed as I lay on my back and threw my head off the edge.

"What's this?" Emma said curiously.

"I'm going to fuck her mouth," Paul answered.

"It's the same principle, but you put him in control. It's hot," I said happily as my lover brought his cock to my lips. Emma instinctively lay down on her back next to me, watching.

I closed my eyes and opened my mouth as Paul steadily drove his cock into my mouth, gave me a second to adjust, then pressed into my throat and started to fuck it as only he could. We had done this a lot since our first "meeting", and he knew how much I loved to surrender control to him until he came directly into my stomach.

"She has to trust me completely. Pixie can't breathe until I let her," Paul said as I adjusted my position slightly. "Watch."

He pulled out, I took a breath, I closed my eyes, and then he drove in. He held himself in place, his entire cock inside me, sliding forward and back slightly as I began to struggle for breath a little, my back arched and my arms flailing. He knew I was okay, I always pressed his legs when I needed an escape, but Emma didn't know that, and she sounded concerned.

"She okay?" she asked, watching me as I opened my eyes, and they started to stream a little.

"She's fine," Paul said calmly, pulling out of my throat and letting me inhale quickly.

I coughed, then smiled at her. "You okay?" she asked.

"Better than okay," I replied, lying back down."It's such a turn-on."

I was about to take Paul back inside my mouth when Emma spoke.

"Let me try!" she said excitedly, rolling from facing me onto her back, dropping her head off the edge of the bed next to mine.

"Okay, but if you need to breathe, just push on Paul's leg gently, and he'll pull back, Okay?"

"Okay," she replied, licking her lips as Paul took a sidestep towards her.

She opened her mouth, and I rolled onto my side, watching Paul slowly slip his cock between her lips until he met resistance. She gagged and arched her back, and he withdrew slightly. She raised her arms behind his legs and gave him a gentle, encouraging pull. He pressed in again, and I saw her adjust, her windpipe swelling once more as he slid his cock inside. He held her there, as he had with me, as she started to writhe beneath him, then pulled out.

"Again," she whispered.

He drove in, holding for longer this time. Emma reached for my hand and squeezed it until he withdrew again. She coughed, wiped her mouth, and then looked up at him.

"Now fuck my mouth like you fuck Pixie's," she whispered.

He held her wrists beside her and leaned over her body a little, then slid his cock back into her willing mouth and began to fuck it, giving her a split second to breathe occasionally as he gave her precisely what she asked him for. I'd never seen it up close before. I was always the recipient. It looked amazing, and Emma took it well. Paul fucked and fucked her, and she just kept encouraging him. Eventually, his breathing changed as her throat massaged his cock.

"Don't come in her throat," I insisted. "Come in her mouth."

"Then we might need to switch things up," he said.

He pulled out, allowing Emma to catch her breath while he climbed onto the bed, and we lay beside him.

"Make him come for you, Nymph. Stay shallow when he does so you have room for it all in your mouth," I whispered.

Emma bent down and continued sucking him eagerly as Paul quickly climaxed. He reached out and gripped her head, holding it in place as she experienced a cock streaming hot semen into her mouth for the first time. Emma moaned as he continued to empty into her, clearly loving every second of it.

"Don't swallow," I said without thinking. "I want some."

Emma slipped her mouth off Paul, slowing her lips and holding his come inside her mouth. She sat up and came over to me, sitting between my legs and wrapping hers around me. She leaned forwards, and with her mouth full, she kissed me deeply.

I recognised his taste, and I loved receiving it from her. We made a mess, as what we didn't swallow between us dripped from our mouths. We cleaned each other's lips, lapping up everything we could get, and then Emma looked down.

"You seem to have Paul's come on your tits, Pixie,"

I looked down. "So do you," I giggled.

"I saw it first," she said, leaning down and licking Paul's semen from my nipples slowly. Then she leaned back, and I buried my face into her chest, lapping up all the spillages.

"You two are insatiable," Paul said, distracting us. We pressed our heads together and smiled at him.

"We're not done yet," Emma said sweetly. "Are we Pixie?"

"Oh, no, Nymph. We're not."

About half an hour after Emma and I had given Paul the oral of his life, we were laying on his bed, still naked and drinking what was left of the Prosecco, while he fetched coffee and snacks from the kitchen.

In all the excitement, we hadn't noticed that it had gone dark outside, and the bedroom had dimmed. I put on a bedside lamp, and we dove under Paul's duvet to keep ourselves warm. Having been mostly naked and horny since about two that afternoon, we hadn't noticed the chill in the room until the inevitable lull in the sexual circus we were involved in.

Paul returned with hot coffee and climbed into the bed between us. We drank our coffees quietly, enjoying the sensual atmosphere. Then as we finished them, Emma and I cuddled up to him, and the three of us dozed off for a while, which gave us all the break we needed.

A few hours later, I was awakened by movement on the bed. I didn't open my eyes initially. I just lay there, listening. I could hear Emma breathing, but it was shallow, rushed. She was letting out the faintest of gentle whimpers. I instantly knew that she was enjoying some one-on-one time with Paul. I wondered who instigated it. Did he wake up horny and choose her over me? Did she wake up horny and want him?

I could have gone into a spiral. I could've wondered if Paul preferred her body to mine. Instead, I listened, happy to share him with her and her with him.

Her moans became muffled. She'd buried her face in the pillow to avoid making too much noise. Were they trying to let me sleep or to have some time alone without me? Again, I could have spiralled, but I didn't.

I opened my eyes a little. The only light in the bedroom came from the slightly open door of the ensuite. It's light on to give Emma and me a path to it in the night if needed. The light bathed the room just enough for me to see their silhouettes.

Emma's face was in the pillow beside me, with her arms under it. She was kneeling, her shapely, beautiful ass pointing skyward as Paul knelt behind her, lapping at her pussy. I lay there silently, enjoying the show.

I know Paul well. I know how his mind works. And having Emma in that position was probably no coincidence. There was something else he wanted to pleasure—something that, earlier in the evening a least, Emma was less sure about.

Sure enough, I watched him put a hand on her ass cheeks and part them slightly as his tongue slid upward slowly and pressed against her ass. She moaned, offering no resistance, so he probed her rear entrance more lavishly with his tongue. I watched, wondering who I wanted to be more right now—him or Emma.

I didn't get a chance to answer my question as Emma pressed her body back onto the bed and rolled over to look at him, panting. I closed my eyes to maintain my illusion of sleep.

"Fuck me the way you fuck Pixie," she whispered. Just hearing her say the words so eagerly and desperately started to turn me on, a warmth growing between my legs.

"You'll be too loud. We'll wake Pix up."

"No, you won't," I whispered, smiling and breaking my cover.

Emma looked across. "How long?"

"Long enough to see him stick his tongue in your ass," I replied, opening my eyes and looking into hers. Emma's beautiful blue eyes were wide, horny, and eager. I looked up at Paul.

"You heard Nymph. Fuck her the way you fuck me."

"It will be my pleasure," he said. "Pass the condoms Pix,"

"No," Emma said softly, looking up at him. "If you don't need them with Pixie, you don't need them with me."

"Em," I said softly.

"It's okay. I'm on the pill. My mum thought it was a good idea before I came to University. It finally turns out it was," she said, smiling.

I reached up to where the condom box stood on Paul's bedside table and picked up his bottle of lube.

"If he is going to give you the full Pixie treatment, you'll be grateful for some of this," I said, flipping the lid and dripping some onto her clit. She wriggled at the cold sensation. I put down the bottle and slid closer to Emma's naked body, sliding my hand between her legs and slowly massaging the lube into her clit and pussy lips. She closed her eyes, delighted with the attention.

"Will it feel different without the condom?" Emma asked.

"Oh, yes. Just wait and see," I replied. "Now, if you will excuse me a moment, I'm just going to make that cock rock hard for you."

Paul was still sitting where he had been while enjoying Emma's pussy and ass. I climbed over to him, and as he knelt on the bed, I knelt directly behind him, putting my legs on either side of his, pressing my body into his back. I slid my hands under his arms, stroked his chest, and slid them downward. I took his growing cock in one hand and slipped my other hand down, massaging his balls gently as I looked over his shoulder, and we both admired the naked beauty before us.

Emma looked up at us, her eyes glistening.

"Isn't she beautiful?" I asked, intentionally loud enough for us all to hear. Emma stared up at me, enjoying being at the centre of our attention.

"She is," Paul replied. Growing hard as I slowly jerked his cock in my hand.

"Those beautiful blue eyes, that face, those breasts, and those amazing legs," I said softly.

Emma smiled. Paul became harder.

"And that perfect pussy," I whispered.

Emma bit her bottom lip and opened her legs for us. Paul's cock was ready, but I didn't want her to have it yet.

"She wants you to fuck her brains out."

I paused.

"And I want you to fuck her so hard she can't breathe between orgasms. Then I want you to come in her beautiful pussy for me so that I clean it out with my tongue," I said seductively, smiling at Emma over his shoulder.

Emma's eyes sparkled, and Paul's cock twitched in my hand.

"But not yet," I said softly.

I let go of Paul's cock and went around in front of him. I bent over slightly, took hold of his cock again, guided it inside my soaking wet pussy and pressed backwards, sliding his length deep inside me. Then I leaned down and pressed my tongue against Emma's clit.

"Fuck," she moaned aloud as Paul grabbed my hips and withdrew. He slammed his cock into me, pressing my tongue harder against her clit. I slid down to check her readiness. I slipped my tongue inside her a little; the taste of Paul's cherry lube and the wetness of her pussy told me that Emma was more than ready.

I looked up into her eyes and smiled.

"Take her. She's ready," I whispered, sliding my pussy off Paul's cock and climbing out of his way.

It killed me to do it. Paul's cock was rock hard and felt as amazing as ever, but it was time for Emma, his Nymph, to experience him how I loved to.

As I climbed off the bed, Paul slid forward between Emma's now almost permanently open and silky smooth legs.

As I walked away, eager to be sitting in the chair and ready to watch before the action began in earnest, I heard Paul speak.

"Let's start slow." I loved Emma's response.

"No, we've done slow. It was great. But now I want rough. Pixie rough,"

She asked for it, to be fair. Paul leaned over and positioned his impressive cock at her entrance and, as he had done with me so many times, drove straight into Emma's tight pussy to the hilt.

She screamed—a loud, high-pitched scream. Within her scream were a few discernable words. "Holy fuck, yes."

Then, Emma did something brave. She looked up into Paul's eyes, and through gritted teeth, she spoke;

"Fuck me like you mean it."

Paul stared down at her as he slowly reached behind him, took hold of her calves and pressed them upward slowly. To Emma's credit, years of gymnastics helped her out. Paul pressed until Emma was practically perfectly folded in two, her ankles on either side of her pretty little face.

She reached up slowly and held them there for him as he put his hands on the bed on either side of her to support his upper body while he pounded her. He was intentionally slow in his preparation, staring deep into her eyes. She was patient, staring back at him, knowing her fate was sealed, and enjoying the patient build-up. Paul withdrew his cock to the tip. Emma took a deep breath. Then Paul gave her precisely what she asked for.

Paul used his entire body weight, probably at least twice that of his tiny Nymph, to slam downward and drive his cock inside her, and he was utterly, utterly relentless. Emma started by screaming a little. Then as the relentless onslaught of Paul's cock in her pussy continued, she simply whimpered or yelped each time his body weight landed on her.

From where I was sitting, it looked incredible, and I hoped to have a video of him doing this to me one day. I knew first-hand that being where Emma was right at that moment quickly turns into an orgasmic blur, so it would be hot to see him doing that to me.

I had warned Emma if you remember, that Paul was likely to switch her around a little. I was surprised at how long he kept her body in that position. But, thinking about it, those beautiful piercing blue eyes must have been at their widest, their wildest, looking up at him from between her perfect little ankles as his cock stretched her almost entirely untouched pussy. If I were him, I would probably have done the same. Eventually, though, he moved her. He slowed and withdrew. Her yelps of pleasure softened as he reached forward, took her left leg from her grasp, lowered it onto the bed, and then straddled it. He leaned her right leg against his upright body, her dainty little foot beside his face as her shapely leg stood perfectly straight against his body. I saw him kiss her ankle, distracting her as he positioned his cock, then he held her ankle tight, pressed in a little, then put his other hand on her thigh and went deep into her once more.

Paul told me later that it was then that Emma's eyes rolled backwards, and she began to shake violently. He struggled to maintain a rhythm inside her despite his strength, such was the enormity of her orgasm.

I didn't notice. Not until Emma regained full consciousness and continued howling with pleasure. Why? I lay back in the chair and hooked my legs over the arms a while back. So that I could play with myself a little and watch. But I was just too horny, so at the point Emma's eyes rolled, I was panting a little myself, thanks to my fingers on my clit and the neck of an empty prosecco bottle in my pussy. Sometimes you need to use what's nearby.

I'm sure you can imagine that in one hard fuck Emma didn't get to experience all of the positions in mine and Paul's usual repertoire. Usually, he would only have his Pixie on tap, so the poor guy's cock didn't have to work quite as hard. Not that he seemed to be complaining.

No, Emma wasn't pressed against the wall and fucked from behind as I so often was, nor was she bent over and made to put her palms on the floor as she tried in vain (believe me, it was impossible) to remain on her feet as he jackhammered his cock into her. She did, over the next five minutes or so, get pulled up onto all fours and took a deep hammering from behind as she came again, screaming, and he bent her over the bed with similar results.

It became evident that, like me, Emma was the type of girl that once she'd reached orgasm unless she had a break, they would keep coming (pardon the pun) in waves.

In the meantime, I'd come on the neck of the Prosecco bottle and maintained it for a while, missing some of the action as I closed my eyes. I was distracted from my solo play by Paul's voice.

"On your back Nymph. I want to look into your eyes when I come in your pussy."

I looked over to see him withdraw from Emma. She was still bent over the bed, her entire body glistening with sweat, as was his. She crawled slowly onto the bed, clearly exhausted, and opened her legs wide. He glanced at me and nodded to Emma.

I removed the bottle from my pussy and sat on the bed in a shot next to Emma. I kissed her deeply as Paul slid his cock into her again. She sighed, unable to concentrate on my kiss. I looked at him.

"Come hard, give her what she craves," I told him.

Emma whimpered happily. Paul started back up slowly. Emma gripped my hand as he increased his speed, his breath changing as he prepared to be the first man to come into her tight young pussy. Paul groaned and withdrew a little, then grabbed her hips and slid into her hard, his body shaking as he pumped his load deep into her. He thrust for a while, making sure, as he so often did with me, that Emma received every drop.

Throughout the experience of Paul's cock pulsing into her, she moaned softly into my ear as I watched him breed her with my head on her chest.

When he'd finished, I sat up, and she looked up at him.

"Okay, Nymph?" he asked, his cock still inside her.

"Oh, fuck," she whispered, smiling.

"I'll take that as a yes. Pixie, there's a beautiful pussy full of come here for you, as requested."

"You okay with this?" I asked Emma, still panting on the bed. As much as I wanted to, it did occur to me that there was a possibility that after the sex she had just had, she might want to sleep. "I'll be gentle."

Emma looked up at me and blinked. "You don't ever have to ask if you can put your head between my legs, Pixie," she replied.

"Then I'll leave you two to it and have a shower," Paul said, withdrawing his cock from Emma slowly, his action creating soft moans of pleasure.

As Paul disappeared into his bathroom, Emma stayed where she was, knees bent, legs open, waiting for me. I knelt briefly between her legs, studying her pussy. It still looked perfect, though now glistening with Paul's come a little. As I leaned down, I noticed that some had made it's way out of her beautiful lips and had slid down to her ass. I had wanted to probe her gorgeous ass with my tongue since I had watched Paul do it to her earlier, and I took my opportunity. I leaned down low, pressed my tongue into her rear opening, and slid upward, scoping up semen as I went. Emma offered no resistance to my tongue pressing against her ass. In fact, she even opened her legs a little further and moaned as I did so. Something for another time, I thought.

I wanted Emma to enjoy me extracting Paul's come from her pussy. I knew she must be sore, as I often was after a session like that with him, so I was gentle, romantic, passionate, and meticulous in my search for everything her pussy was prepared to let me have. The rest I was happy for it to keep as a souvenir of her first hot fuck. She loved running her hands through my hair and moaning softly as I worked. This whole weekend had been a bonding experience for me and Emma. But this act of passion, as I submissively worshipped her come-filled pussy, was the peak of our time together so far.

As I finished, reluctantly, I slid up Emma's body and lay on her. She put her arms around my neck and kissed me slowly, tasting his come and her own on my lips. She meant that kiss. We both did. It wasn't an act of sexual desire or passion. It was a kiss filled with newly discovered affection. I rolled off her and gently encouraged her onto her side, then sidled up against her tired body, spooning her naked body and stroking her arm softly as I heard her breathing change, and she quickly drifted off to sleep.

I was drifting myself as Paul came out of his bathroom, naked. She looked over at us, entwined together in the dim light, and shook his head in disbelief. I can't say I blamed him. I was a little, too.

He silently climbed onto the bed behind me. He spooned me, his warm, masculine, comparatively massive frame against my back, contrasting with the petite, soft, feminine beauty against my chest. Both felt perfect.

As he slid a leg across mine, I slowly stroked his soft cock.

"I bet this is exhausted," I whispered.

"For now," he replied, kissing my shoulder and leaning against me. "Let's see how it feels in the morning."

I smiled and let sleep overcome me, nestled between two perfect, naked lovers.

When I awoke the following day, Emma was gone. I reached behind me, and so was Paul. I lay there for a second, wondering where they were, and then I heard the toilet flush in the ensuite and the shower turn on. I smiled as Emma started singing to herself, clearly happy. The front door closed, and I heard Paul throw his car keys into the little bowl atop his drawers in the hall. He'd been out, but what for?

I rolled over and looked at the clock. Ten in the morning. Late for me. But not surprising. I needed a shower myself. I wondered.

I rubbed my eyes and got up, strolling over to the ensuite and tried the door. Emma had left it unlocked. I looked around the door to see the steam-obscured silhouette of her shapely body behind the condensated glass, her back to me.

I closed the door behind me, approached the shower, and opened the door timidly. Emma turned and looked at me. She giggled and reached out a hand, pulling me inside as I closed the door.

"Hey, beautiful," she said softly, putting her arms around my neck and kissing me briefly.

"Hey," I replied, stepping into the water and pressing my body against hers.

She lifted a leg and wrapped it around me as she leaned in for a long lingering kiss, pulling our bodies together. I held her tight, savouring the moment.

She leaned back and looked into my eyes. "So, who's washing who first?"

I picked up the bottle of body wash that Paul had bought me to leave at his house. Some things he and I got up to meant I had to shower a few times during each stay, but that's another story.

She turned her back to me. I spent an age gently washing her back and shoulders silently before kneeling behind her and attending to her beautifully soft, pale white legs. It was erotic but passionate. Eventually, she turned, and I slowly cleaned the rest of her body—every inch. I stood slowly, pleased with myself. She kissed me and took the bottle.

"My turn," she whispered. Emma was no less diligent in her attention, and by the time she had finished, she had touched every single part of me. Something that no other person had. We washed each other's hair, keeping our bodies close. Then as we had finished, Emma pressed me against the wall one last time. The warm water ran down our bodies as she cupped my breast, slid her legs between mine, and kissed me. She leaned back.

"Paul will have sorted breakfast by now, I imagine," she said, turning off the shower. "Come on." She took my hand, and we went into the bedroom, drying ourselves and our hair and combing it straight before popping on our Pixie dresses and breezing hand in hand down to the kitchen.

Paul was standing leaning against the countertop, looking refreshed and very handsome. It felt normal as we approached him and leaned against his body. He kissed me first this time, then, after she waited patiently, Emma. We sat at the kitchen table, covered with pastries, juices, fruit, everything two young girls could need to replace their sexually burnt energy. He joined us at the table with a coffee and one each for me and Emma.

"So, what time do you two ladies need to leave?" he asked, reaching for a croissant.

"We should try to see my mum and dad before our train, so we should probably be home by one," I said gloomily. The realisation that our sexual bubble would soon need to burst.

Emma saw my disappointment and gently stroked her bare foot up the inside of my leg under the table, causing me to look up at her.

"I've been thinking. If you want to, you two can always invite me again sometime. I mean, I know this is your thing. But it's been a lot of fun."

Paul and I looked at each other, sharing a smile.

"I thought this was just practice for your new sex life with Adrian?" I teased.

"And yet, it turned into so much more," she said, her eyes glistening. She looked down, stirring her coffee. "You know, I feel a bit guilty. I haven't thought about Adrian once since I've been here till you mentioned him, Pixie."

"Well, you have been pretty busy, Nymph," Paul said, reminding her of his pet name for her. She bit her bottom lip as she looked down into her coffee still. "It has only been a month and two actual dates, just the two of us."

I watched as she thought things through. I knew exactly what she was thinking, as I would have thought it too. She also did exactly what I would have done next and changed the subject. She picked up her coffee and looked across at me.

"So, we need to leave here in a few hours," she said softly. "Anything you want to do before we leave?"

It was my turn to bite my lip. "Well, now you mention it, there might be one thing."

"Does it involve that cute little ass of yours?" she asked.

I looked up at him, gooey-eyed at the mere thought of him inside my ass.

"I'll take that as a yes," Emma giggled. "Good, 'cause I want to watch."

"You two had better hurry and finish your breakfasts then," Paul said happily. "I'll be upstairs, waiting." He strolled out of the room, leaving us alone. I picked up my coffee, staring across the table at Emma as I finished it. Even with no make-up and slightly damp hair, she was still the most beautiful creature. Having tasted her and been with her, I desperately wanted her again.

"What are you thinking?" she asked seductively.

"I'm thinking I want a strap-on, a box of dildos, some body chocolate, and twenty-four hours alone with you."

She looked at me and smiled, her foot rising inside my leg under the table again. This time she continued upward, and I parted my legs slightly as it slid toward my pussy. She pressed her toe gently against my clit, and I nearly dropped my mug as I moaned.

"Then let's do that. Soon," Emma said sweetly. "But first, I need to get you upstairs so I can watch that older man of yours slide his cock into your ass."

"When you see, you'll want to try," I said softly.

"Probably," she replied, fluttering her eyelids at me. "But not today. This morning is all about you, Pixie."

She put her mug down and stood, holding out her hand. I took it, and she pulled me slowly to my feet. She pulled me close and kissed me, a welcome distraction to allow her to slide her hand around my back and onto my ass. She squeezed a cheek, digging her nails in ever so slightly.

"Come on. Let's get you fucked."

She led me by the hand and took me upstairs to Paul's bedroom, where he was sitting on his bed in only his boxer shorts, waiting for me. Emma led me to stand in front of him, facing her. In a complete reversal to the day before, she slowly undressed me, insisting on slowly opening each button on my dress rather than sliding it back over my head. It was both erotic and sweet—the exact mirror of what I'd done before I'd given her to him yesterday. I struggled to keep still, delighted to have her undressing me and excited for what would come next. She went behind me and turned me to face Paul. Then she peeled off my dress.

"How do you want her?" Emma asked.

"On her knees, bent over the bed, please, Nymph," Paul said, realising Emma had taken control. I immediately surrendered it to her willingly.

She took my hand as Paul stood up and took off his boxers. His cock was semi-hard. I wondered who would be charged with standing it up this morning. She led me over to his bed, put her hand on my shoulder, and I knelt, flicking my long brown hair down the side of my naked body. She knelt beside me and pressed me forward onto the duvet, then slid her hand down my back slowly and across my ass. Her fingertips lowered and stroked my pussy. She slipped them inside me a little.

"Someone's already horny," she whispered, removing her fingers and letting me watch as she licked them before me.

My face must have said it all. Emma looked up at Paul, standing and stroking his cock, watching us.

"Mind if I taste her first?"

"Be my guest," he replied.

Emma went around behind me and bent down, slipping her beautiful soft tongue between my pussy lips and gently lapping at them, making me shudder and moan with delight. I heard her giggle, then felt her tongue slip out of me and upward, probing my ass. I panted as she explored deeper and deeper. I glanced up at Paul, his eyes wild with excitement at seeing Emma preparing me for him. He turned his back and picked up the cherry lube.

"Massage some of this into her for me, Nymph. It helps her take a good seeing to." Emma withdrew a little as Paul drizzled the lube onto my opening, and Emma's fingers started to massage it in.

"Get in deep, Nymph. She'll like that."

Emma giggled again. "Okay," and she carefully slid a finger inside me. Given her perfectly manicured fingernail led the way, it's a testament to the care she took that I didn't feel it. Or the second. Or the

127

third. Granted, three of her dainty little fingers equated to about the same as two of Paul's, but they both seemed impressed at how I moaned in ecstasy as she slid her fingers deep into me.

"I think she's ready," Emma said to Paul. "Are you?"

I was writhing on the bed, my face in the duvet under Emma's erotic spell, and didn't see. But I heard.

"Oh, just let me check," then a muffling sound as Paul stuffed his cock into Emma's willing mouth briefly.

"Yeah, I think so."

I heard the bottle of lube land on the bed next to me. That was usually the sign Paul had prepared his cock for deep anal penetration. Emma withdrew her fingers.

"I'll just be over here," she said sweetly as Paul squatted behind me and slowly slipped himself into my ass.

It felt, as it always did, overwhelming. Paul never went shallow and waited for me to adjust. Not any more. He knew I could handle every last millimetre of his cock in my ass and made sure I did right from the outset.

I heard Emma gasp and giggle as he withdrew a little and thrust harder and harder. We had all worked out that Emma had a naughty playful side, but just how naughty came to light as she climbed onto the bed and opened her legs on either side of my head. She was close enough for me to smell her beautiful scent but too far away to taste it. I looked up as Paul slammed his cock harder and harder into my ass, moaning and wailing loudly as I felt his manhood relentlessly invading me. Emma's pussy was so aching close to my face. She lifted her dress a little and smiled at me gleefully as she slipped her fingers inside herself before my eyes. She tilted her head back and moaned as she pleasured herself.

I can only imagine what Paul was thinking. He loved taking me anally. He often commented on how gorgeous my tight little ass looked and felt as he slid inside it. Today he had the added sight of Emma masturbating for us both as he pounded into me.

No surprise, then, that Paul didn't last quite as long as he usually might. There had been times on previous visits when I'd had him take me in my back passage in multiple positions before he came. But not today. I stayed as I was, on my knees bent over his bed, staring longingly between Emma's legs as he started to grunt and upped his already feverish pace.

"Are you going to come in Pixie's ass?" Emma asked sweetly.

"Any fucking second," Paul grunted.

"Oooh, let me see," she said, hurrying off the bed and standing beside him as she watched his cock repeatedly disappear inside my tightness.

"Do it. Pixie needs it. Come in her," she squealed happily.

Let's be honest. Paul didn't need encouragement. He never needed encouragement to come inside my body. But having her bouncing around excitedly was great. He grabbed my hips tighter and lifted me off the floor as he drove his cock deep into my ass one last time, then held me there in the air as he drained himself deep into my back passage.

"Fucking hell," Emma exclaimed.

Paul withdrew slowly and watched as I let my ass gape for the two of them a little. Emma was fascinated. I slowly adjusted, and as my entrance closed, a little of his semen dripped out and down across my pussy.

"Oops. Let me help with that," Emma said, bending down and licking my pussy clean. I could have cried with pleasure. She sat back.

"You missed a bit," Paul said teasingly, wondering how far she'd take things. She didn't miss a beat.

"Oh yeah, I did, didn't I?" she said.

I honestly thought she was joking until I felt her beautiful soft mouth close onto my ass and her tongue begin to clean the residual come from my opening. She even explored a little deeper and moaned as loudly as I did. The sheer taboo of her actions turning us both on beyond belief.

"Done?" I heard her ask.

"Good girl," Paul replied. "It seems there's more to come from you yet."

"Try me," she said sweetly as I sat beside her. She kissed me briefly, then glanced at the clock.

"I guess we had better think about becoming Emma and P again and returning to your parents."

I sighed. "I've loved this."

"Me too," Emma replied.

"Me three," Paul said.

I turned to Emma, knowing I didn't need to check with Paul before I asked. "Fancy doing this again sometime?"

She smiled excitedly. "Are you joking? Any time at all."

I looked up at Paul. "What do you reckon? Fancy having two mouths, two pussys and an ass to fuck regularly?" I asked.

"Two asses," Emma added. "I've got to try that," she said eagerly.

"Two asses," I said, smiling, correcting myself.

"Like you need to ask," he replied, strolling into his ensuite and turning on the shower.

An hour later, back in our skin-tight jeans, boots and tight tops, Emma and I kissed Paul goodbye and strolled, hand in hand, back to my house. We spent an hour with my parents, telling them all about the fictitious night we'd had at a nightclub in town and the friend's house we'd stayed at. I even set up our next trip home in two weeks. My parents seemed to like Emma, which wasn't a surprise. Everybody loves Emma.

I pulled my phone from my bag as we sat on the train back to the University. Emma was on hers a fair bit, her modelling had garnered her thousands of followers on Instagram, and she liked to keep them entertained, but I rarely bothered with mine. As I opened the screen, I had notification after notification. I opened Instagram, and my followers had increased by nearly two thousand in the last few hours, and I had thousands of likes.

"What the?" I said, mowing my way through the notifications.

Emma laughed. "Oh, yeah, sorry. I meant to say."

I found the source. While I was still asleep that morning, Emma posted the picture she had taken of us in our Pixie dresses the afternoon before, standing seductively together. She'd tagged me and given it a caption.

"My goddess. My girl. Meet the beautiful Miss P xx."

I looked up at her and smiled.

"Well, you and I are going to spend a lot of time together, with and without Paul, so the fans should get to know you. I suspect you'll be in a lot of my pictures. And judging by their reaction, you're popular." She smiled and took my hand. "Not that it's a surprise. You're stunning, P."

I looked down, both embarrassed and flattered simultaneously. "Now," Emma said, "let's see about ordering those dildos and that strap-on we'll need to keep us occupied until we get to Paul's next."

Don't miss out!

Visit the website below and you can sign up to receive emails whenever P.T. Brown publishes a new book. There's no charge and no obligation.

https://books2read.com/r/B-A-BVXX-ZNMMC

BOOKS 2 READ

Connecting independent readers to independent writers.

Did you love *Confessions of an Erotic Author Part One: The University Years*? Then you should read *Mary's Awakening*[1] by P.T. Brown!

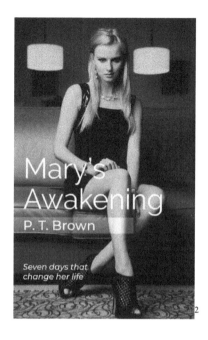

[2]

Starting her second year at uni, Mary's "arrangement" with Elliot, her friend-with-benefits, is fun but getting a bit predictable. She yearns for something new and exciting, but isn't really doing anything about it. She doesn't feel she needs to. For a 20 year old Uni student sex is practically a vital food group, and something will come along eventually.

A chance (and initially quite embarrassing) encounter with Richard, the handsome, older guy who just moved in to her shared house gives her something exciting to think about. She gathers up her confidence and explores the possibility of some no-strings sex with the handsome stranger. Over the next week, her boundaries are pushed, her

1. https://books2read.com/u/4j59X5

2. https://books2read.com/u/4j59X5

body explored, and her eyes opened to things she never knew possible, and as it turns out, she really rather likes them...

This book is reaonably graphic erotic fiction and is intended for those over the age of 18.

All characters are ficticious and are over the age of 18.

Read more at https://pt-brown.com/.

Also by P.T. Brown

Confessions of an Erotic Author
Confessions of an Erotic Author Part One: The University Years

Four couples get kinky
Four Couples Get Kinky, Part One: Exploration

Mary's Erotic Adventures
Mary's Awakening
Mary's Evolution

Standalone
Sophie's Hotwife Adventures

Watch for more at https://pt-brown.com/.

About the Author

P.T.Brown is an author of erotic fiction, with a full-time career doing something completely different.

Most stories feature strong women, who choose what they want, when, and from whom.

Some scenes are left a little to the imagination, others are *very much* not.

Read more at https://pt-brown.com/.

Milton Keynes UK
Ingram Content Group UK Ltd.
UKHW012308160823
426962UK00004B/212